BODYGUARD

Book 5 : Ambush

Also by Chris Bradford

The Bodyguard series
Book 1: Recruit
Book 2: Hostage
Book 3: Hijack
Book 4: Ransom
Book 5: Ambush
Book 6: Survival

Book 5: Ambush

Chris Bradford

Philomel Books

PHILOMEL BOOKS
an imprint of Penguin Random House LLC
375 Hudson Street, New York, NY 10014

Copyright © 2015, 2017 by Chris Bradford.
First American edition published by Philomel Books in 2017. Adapted from
Ambush, originally published in the United Kingdom by Puffin Books in 2015.
Penguin supports copyright. Copyright fuels creativity, encourages diverse
voices, promotes free speech, and creates a vibrant culture. Thank you for
buying an authorized edition of this book and for complying with copyright
laws by not reproducing, scanning, or distributing any part of it in any form
without permission. You are supporting writers and allowing Penguin to
continue to publish books for every reader.

Philomel Books is a registered trademark of Penguin Random House LLC.

Library of Congress Cataloging-in-Publication Data is available upon request.
Printed in the United States of America.
ISBN 9781524737054
10 9 8 7 6 5 4 3 2 1

American edition edited by Brian Geffen.
American edition design by Jennifer Chung.
Text set in 11-point Palatino Nova.
This is a work of fiction. Names, characters, places, and incidents either are
the product of the author's imagination or are used fictitiously, and any
resemblance to actual persons, living or dead, businesses, companies, events,
or locales is entirely coincidental.

In honor of the HGC—
you know who you are!

"The best bodyguard is the one nobody notices."

With the rise of teen stars, the intense media focus on celebrity families and a new wave of millionaires and billionaires, adults are no longer the only target for hostage-taking, blackmail and assassination—kids are too.

That's why they need specialized protection . . .

GUARDIAN

Guardian is a secret close-protection organization that differs from all other security outfits by training and supplying only young bodyguards.

Known as guardians, these highly skilled kids are more effective than the typical adult bodyguard, who can easily draw unwanted attention. Operating invisibly as a child's constant companion, a guardian provides the greatest possible protection for any high-profile or vulnerable young target.

In a life-threatening situation, a **guardian** is the final ring of defense.

PREVIOUSLY ON BODYGUARD . . .

Following his first assignment protecting the U.S. president's daughter, Guardian recruit Connor Reeves is tasked with keeping safe twin sisters aboard a luxury yacht in the Indian Ocean . . .

Jason shot Connor an envious glance. "You've landed a cushy assignment," he said. "Must be your reward for saving the president's daughter."

"You think so?" replied Connor, recalling the difficulties he'd faced protecting just one Principal. "I figure twins mean twice the trouble."

———

Connor isn't wrong in his assumption. Even before they set sail, Chloe and Emily are the targets of an attack . . .

"Watch out!" Connor bawled at the top of his lungs. But Chloe just stood there, wide-eyed, like a rabbit caught in the headlights.

The Rollerblader, a dome-headed black man with wrap-around sunglasses, sped toward her with the force of a battering ram. With only seconds to react, Ling discarded the surfboard and launched herself into his path. Small as she was for a guardian, she collided hard enough to knock him off course. They both struck the concrete sea wall and toppled over the side.

——— ———

But the mugging is nothing compared to the plans of a ruthless pirate gang intent on hijacking the yacht . . .

"What have we got here?" muttered Big Mouth as he hefted out a brand-new rocket-propelled grenade launcher . . . and took aim at the rusted cargo ship in the bay.

"Look out for that old fisherman," warned Bucktooth as he eyed the formidable weapon with a mix of awe and fear.

"*He's* the one who should look out." With a crooked grin, Big Mouth pressed the trigger.

The rocket *whooshed* out of the launcher and scorched over the waves . . . and struck the cargo ship behind the fisherman. There was a deep howl of twisting metal as a massive explosion ripped through the hull.

"Did you see *that*?" whooped Big Mouth, dancing a jig on the beach. "These babies are tank-busters!"

——— ———

As the pirates close in on their prey, Connor and the yacht's crew are forced to fight back . . .

Blasts like thunder echoed off the blood-smeared glass as Brad fired his shotgun in angry retaliation. But the pirates showed no sign of retreat. Bullets ripped through the air, and the roar of their outboard motors buzzed like angry wasps.

Without warning, a grappling hook latched itself to the port-side rail. Connor saw the line go taut. The pirates were boarding the *Orchid*.

———

With the yacht now under their command, the pirates imprison the crew and demand a multi-million-dollar ransom from Chloe and Emily's wealthy father . . .

The girls shrank back from the pirate as he crouched beside them.

"Don't worry, Emily," soothed Spearhead, brushing a calloused finger along her soft cheek. "If your father pays up, you'll be back home in no time."

———

As the deadline looms, the pirates grow more blood-thirsty . . .

Spearhead's hand lashed out like a viper, his knuckles catching the captain hard across the jaw.

"Don't ever lie to me again," snarled Spearhead as Captain Locke reeled from the blow, his split lip gushing fresh blood. "I know for a fact that this yacht has a range of four thousand nautical miles. Start the engines, NOW!"

———

But there's a flaw in their plan. The pirates didn't count on Connor Reeves being aboard . . .

One look at the sheer terror and despair on Emily and Chloe's faces spurred Connor to act. He was their only hope. And, although the odds were stacked against him, it was his duty to protect the girls . . . no matter what it took.

Now Connor embarks on his next heart-stopping assignment . . .

PROLOGUE

No Mercy shifted the AK-47 assault rifle in his grip. His hands were slick with sweat, and the weapon was heavy and cumbersome. The jungle around him pulsed with danger, each and every murky shadow hiding a potential enemy. The sun beat down from the African sky above, but its scorching rays struggled to penetrate the dense canopy running wild along Burundi's northern border. Instead the day's heat was slowly yet steadily absorbed, like a pressure cooker, turning the jungle into a living hell.

Clouds of mosquitoes buzzed in the humid air, and monkeys chattered fearfully in the treetops as No Mercy advanced through the bush alongside his brothers-in-arms. No Mercy was dying for a drink. But he wouldn't stop—*couldn't* stop—until the general gave the order. So he was forced to lick the sweat from his upper lip in a vain attempt to ease his thirst.

As he trekked toward the rendezvous point, ever watchful

for booby traps and old civil-war mines, No Mercy became aware that the monkeys in the trees had gone quiet. In fact, the whole jungle had fallen silent. Only the faint inescapable drone of insects remained.

The general held up a closed fist and the troop halted. Scanning the dense vegetation for any sign of a threat, No Mercy saw nothing besides towering tree trunks, green vines and thick palm fronds. Then out from behind a tree stepped a white man.

No Mercy thrust his AK-47 at him, his finger primed on the trigger.

The white man, his skin more ivory gray than flesh white, didn't move a muscle. With unblinking eyes, he surveyed the band of rebel soldiers in mismatching uniforms and international aid–distributed T-shirts, along with their aging and rusted weapons. Finally his unflinching glare fell upon No Mercy pointing the AK-47 at his chest.

To No Mercy, the white man was something almost alien, totally out of place in the heart of the jungle. Dressed in a spotless olive-green shirt, cargo pants and black combat boots, he didn't seem affected by the stifling heat at all. He wasn't out of breath, let alone sweating. Even the mosquitoes appeared to be giving him a wide berth. The stranger seemed as cold-blooded and inhuman as a lizard.

No Mercy kept the barrel of his assault rifle targeted on the man's chest. His finger itched to pull the trigger. Just one word, even the slightest nod, from the general and he would blast the man away in a hailstorm of bullets. That's how he'd earned his warrior name, "No Mercy," for killing without remorse or pity.

General Pascal stepped forward from among his band of soldiers. As intimidating and large as a silverback gorilla, the Burundian general was a head taller than the white man. He wore army fatigues and a beret as red as fresh blood. His dark pockmarked face sent shudders of fear through the local villagers who knew him, and his fists bore the calloused scars of countless beatings that he'd personally inflicted upon those same villagers.

"Dr. Livingstone, I presume?" said the general, his pencil-thin mustache curling up into an unexpected and disarming smile.

"You have a sense of humor, General," the white man replied without any trace of having one himself. "Now tell your boy soldier to lower his gun before he gets himself killed."

No Mercy bristled at the insult. He might be fifteen, but age meant nothing when you had the authority of a firearm.

The general waved at him to stand down. Reluctantly No Mercy did as he was ordered, pouting his lower lip in a sulk. The AK-47 hung limp from its strap, looking like an oversized yet deadly toy against the young boy's side.

"Do you have the stone?" the stranger asked.

General Pascal snorted. "You white men! Always straight

down to business." He looked the man up and down. "On that point, where are my guns?"

"Stone first."

"Don't you trust me, Mr. Gray?"

The white man didn't respond. This unsettled No Mercy even more. The fact that the stranger showed no fear in the presence of the general made him either unbelievably brave or unbelievably stupid. General Pascal had hacked the hands off people for lesser crimes than failing to answer a direct question. Then No Mercy was struck by a terrible and chilling thought: this Mr. Gray was somehow *more* dangerous than the general himself.

General Pascal nodded to No Mercy. "Show him the stone."

No Mercy pulled out a grimy cloth bag from the pocket of his oversized camo jacket. He passed it to Mr. Gray, careful not to touch the man's ashen skin. Mr. Gray emptied the contents of the bag into his hand. A large rock with a pale pink hue fell into his open palm. Taking out an eyeglass, he inspected the rather unassuming stone. After some consideration, he declared, "This is of poor quality."

The general let out a booming laugh that shattered the silence of the jungle. "Don't take me for a fool, Mr. Gray. You and I both know this is a very valuable *pink* diamond."

Mr. Gray made the pretense of reevaluating the stone, the power play between the two men all part of the negotiation process. He sighed with some reluctance. "It'll cover your first shipment of weapons," he agreed, then casually added, "Are there more where this came from?"

The general graced him with another of his disarming smiles. "More than you could dream of."

"Have you secured the area where the diamonds are located?"

"Not yet," admitted the general. "But with your guns we will."

Mr. Gray pocketed the stone. "Equilibrium will supply the weapons you need on the condition that once you've seized power, they're granted sole mining rights. Agreed?"

"Agreed," said General Pascal, offering his meaty slab of a hand.

Seemingly loath to take it, Mr. Gray nonetheless extended his own hand.

No Mercy watched the two men shake on the deal. Then his heart leaped in surprise as the jungle erupted with the roar of engines. Two immense military trucks bulldozed their way along an overgrown dirt track. Their rear trailers contained an armory of brand-new AK-47s, Browning heavy machine guns, rocket-propelled grenades, mortars and box upon box of ammunition.

"Double-cross us," warned Mr. Gray over the thunder of engine noise, "and your civil war will be nothing compared with what we'll do to you and your men."

Still smiling, the general replied, "Same goes for you, my friend, same for you and yours."

"Then we are in business," replied Mr. Gray, melting back into the jungle.

1

Connor was violently awakened by a bag being thrust over his head. As he gasped for breath, the thick black fabric smothering all light, strong hands pinned his arms and legs behind his back. He fought to free himself. But plastic zip ties were quickly fastened around his wrists and ankles, binding him tightly.

"Let me go!" he cried, thrashing wildly in a desperate bid to escape. Wrenched from a deep sleep, his mind was a whirl of confusion and blind panic. Lashing out, his heel struck one of his captors, and he heard a grunt of pain.

More hands seized Connor, yanking him upright. As he was hauled from the room, his sneakers dragging across the carpet, he screamed, "HELP! SOMEONE HELP ME!"

But no one answered his call, his cries muffled by the bag.

All of a sudden Connor was hit by a blast of ice-cold air as his captors bundled him outside. Heart pounding and body trembling from the shock of the attack, Connor knew that if he was to survive this ordeal, he had to get a grip on himself. During his bodyguard training in hostage survival, he'd learned that the first thirty minutes of any abduction were the most dangerous. The kidnappers were on edge and highly volatile.

Although it goes against every human instinct, his instructor Jody had explained, *this is the time to stay calm and stay sharp. Be aware of anything that could provide a clue to your whereabouts or your kidnappers' identity.*

Feet crunched on gravel. *Three sets,* Connor noted, trying in some small way to take control of the situation. He heard the trunk of a car being opened. A moment later he was dumped in the back and the trunk was slammed shut with an ominous *thunk.*

No, it isn't a car, Connor corrected himself. He'd been *lifted,* not dropped into the luggage compartment. The deep throaty rumble of a powerful diesel engine confirmed his suspicions. *It's a 4×4 truck.*

Wheels spun on gravel as the vehicle roared away. His body was flung around, and Connor's head struck the rear panel with a crunch. Stars burst before his eyes and pain flared in his skull. Any last vestiges of grogginess were wiped out in an instant.

Someone must have seen me being taken, thought Connor, his mind now sharp. *Someone will raise the alert.*

The wheels hit concrete, likely turning onto a road. The

vehicle banked left before accelerating away fast. With the bag still over his head, Connor attempted to visualize the route his abductors were taking. He carefully counted off the seconds before the next turn.

Sixty-seven . . . sixty-eight . . . sixty-nine . . . The 4×4 took a hard right. Connor began counting again, building up a crude map in his head. He felt the vehicle rise and fall as they passed over a small bridge. He continued his count . . . *twenty-four . . . twenty-five . . . twenty-six . . .*

Connor was totally baffled by his abduction. Usually it was the Principal, the person he was assigned to protect, who was the target for a kidnapping. Surely his captors had made a mistake. Grabbed the wrong person. Besides, he wasn't even on an official mission. Then an uncomfortable truth struck Connor: perhaps his kidnappers had indeed snatched the *right* person.

Crumpled in a heap against the rear panel, Connor shifted position to create a space for his hands. The ties around his wrists and ankles were digging painfully into his flesh, cutting off circulation. He tried to pull a hand free, but the zip ties were heavy-duty, and the plastic just cut deeper into his skin. However hard he strained, they simply wouldn't break.

At a count of forty-seven, the vehicle swung right. Then barely ten seconds later bore left. And soon after that left again. By the sixth turn, Connor's mental map had become a confused mess. It seemed like the 4×4 was going in circles, as if his captors were purposely trying to disorient him. Connor now tried to listen above the noise of the road for any conversation in the vehicle. He hoped to gain some insight into his abductors' identity: *accent, language, gender, even a name.* But they all stayed disturbingly silent. From this Connor deduced they were professionals. They had to be to break into Guardian HQ undetected.

Maybe my kidnapping's connected with a previous mission?

The best he could hope for was that his captors intended to ransom him. That way he'd be worth more to them alive than dead. But if they wanted to interrogate him, or use him as a pawn in some political or religious protest, then he'd likely be killed. In that case he would risk an escape attempt.

Whatever his abductors' intentions, he needed to find out as soon as possible—his life could depend upon it.

The 4×4 ground to a halt and the engine was switched off. The back door opened, and he was manhandled out of the vehicle. A gusting wind sent a chill through his body, his T-shirt offering little protection against the winter freeze. Gripped tightly on either side by his captors, Connor detected the faintest trace of perfume through the bag. Was one of the abductors a woman?

"Where are you taking me?" asked Connor, his voice now steady and calm, hoping that the woman would respond.

But his kidnappers remained tight-lipped as they escorted him away from the 4×4. They moved briskly, not allowing

Connor to find his feet. He heard the soft swish of a door sliding open, a welcoming warmth embraced him, and the ground changed from concrete to cushioned carpet. As he was led deeper into the building, Connor caught the aroma of frying onions and the distant clatter of pots and pans. Heading away from what he presumed was a kitchen, he was dragged several more paces before being shoved into a chair. Its hard wooden slats dug painfully against his bound hands, but at least he could plant his feet on the floor. Connor tried to sit up straight to maintain some dignity before his anonymous enemies, at the same time readying himself to spring into action at the first opportunity.

The place he'd been brought to was oddly quiet, indicating that other people were there with him.

When nobody spoke, Connor demanded, "Who are you? What do you want with me?"

"It's not about what we want," a man's voice replied. "It's about what *you* want."

2

The bag was whipped off Connor's head. Squinting from the glare of an overhead spotlight, Connor discovered that he was sitting at a long glass table set for dinner. Disoriented by the unexpected surroundings, it took him a moment to register the people with him.

"Surprise! Happy birthday!" chorused Alpha team.

Connor stared openmouthed at his fellow guardians. Charley, Amir, Ling, Jason, Marc and Richie were seated on either side of the table. At the opposite end were Colonel Black and his close-protection instructors, Jody, Steve and Bugsy.

"What the . . . ?" Connor exclaimed. He didn't know whether to feel relieved, overjoyed or downright furious.

Colonel Black's craggy face broke into a rare grin. "Glad you could join us."

Connor was now lost for words. He'd honestly believed he was doomed to some terrorist prison cell or, worse, a torturous death. Not a fancy restaurant on the border of the Brecon Beacons in Wales.

Beaming a smile at him, Charley passed across a menu. "So what do you want?" she asked.

Connor barely glanced at the menu, still reeling from the shock of their deception.

"You almost wet yourself with fright!" Ling said, laughing.

This remark snapped Connor out of his daze. "No, I didn't! I was still in control."

"Yeah, about as in control as a turkey on Christmas," snickered Jason.

"Well, I knew I'd been taken in a 4×4 and driven no more than fifteen minutes from HQ. I also figured out that there were at least three kidnappers and one of them was a woman." He glanced over at Jody, who was dressed in a black leather jacket, her dark brown hair tied back in a ponytail.

"Really?" said Jody, unfazed. "How so?"

"Your perfume gave you away."

She raised an eyebrow in admiration. "Then it appears you *were* keeping a cool head. A good thing for a body-guard."

"You're definitely one slippery fish, Connor," admitted Bugsy, the bald-headed surveillance instructor, rubbing his stubbled jaw where Connor's heel had connected. "I'm just glad we managed to restrain you first; otherwise we'd never have gotten you in the back of the Range Rover."

Connor felt some dignity return, knowing that he'd at least proved himself in the situation, even if he hadn't been able to save himself. And now, with the shock fading, he began to see the funny side.

"Well, it's one birthday surprise I won't forget in a hurry! And your little prank has certainly taught me not to fall asleep in the common room again after a night shift," he announced with a laugh. Standing, he turned and presented his bound hands. "Now will someone please get me out of these zip ties?"

Amir rose to help, but the colonel shook his head and waved for him to sit back down.

Connor's brow furrowed. "But how am I going to open my birthday gifts?" he asked in a mock plea.

"With difficulty," Colonel Black said flatly. "*Unless* you can free yourself."

Connor eyed the colonel, incredulous at the suggestion. "You're kidding me, right? I can't break these zip ties. Believe me, I've already tried." He parted his hands to show the red welts on his wrists as proof of his efforts.

"Then it's time you learned how," said the colonel. He directed a nod toward Steve, Alpha team's unarmed combat instructor. At six foot two and built like a tank, the ex–British Special Forces soldier towered over everyone as he got up from his chair. Holding out his sledgehammer hands to Jody, the muscles in his forearms rippling like black waves, he waited while she produced a heavy-duty zip tie and fastened his wrists together.

"The best way to defeat any type of restraint is to analyze how it works," Steve explained. "Zip ties consist of a grooved nylon strip and a ratchet with tiny teeth housed in a small open casing. The weak point, therefore, is the ratchet. So that's where you have to direct any force."

Taking the zip tie in his teeth, Steve adjusted the locking mechanism so that it was positioned midway between his wrists. Then in one fluid motion he raised his hands above his head and came down hard in an arc onto his torso, chicken-winging his arms at the same time. The zip tie pinged off like a rubber band. "There you go. It's that easy."

"*C'est façile pour vous,*" said Marc, then switching from French to English, added, "You're built like the Terminator."

"Yeah, and Connor's arms are behind his back," Amir pointed out.

Steve shrugged. "Same principle applies. Just bend over and bring your hands down against your hips at the same time as you pull your arms apart. Besides, it's about technique and speed, not strength."

Adjusting the zip tie's position, then bending over, Connor followed his instructor's technique. A second later his hands were free. Until that point he'd been pulling and yanking at his restraint when all he needed to do was apply a single strike at the right angle. He shook the blood back into his hands. "That's impressive. But what about my ankles?"

Steve nodded to the dining table. "You've got a steak knife. What more do you need?"

"But what if you don't happen to be in a restaurant?" asked Jason as Connor cut himself loose.

"Then, if you've replaced your shoelaces with paracord as I've recommended, you can use your laces as a friction saw."

Ling jumped up and presented her hands. "That looks like fun. Let me have a go."

"A sucker for punishment?" Steve grinned, taking a spare zip tie from Jody and wrapping it around Ling's wrists.

"Ow! Not *that* tight," Ling squealed as the instructor yanked on the strip.

"The tighter it is, the easier to defeat the locking mechanism," Steve replied with zero pity.

"Good luck, Ling!" called out Jason, biting into a bread roll. "You're going to need it!"

Ling narrowed her half-moon eyes at him, then raised her hands above her head. Despite her slender physique, she broke apart the zip tie on her first attempt.

"Who needs muscles, eh?" she remarked with a ceremonial bow toward Jason.

"My turn now," said Amir, springing to his feet.

This time Steve tied Amir's hands behind his back. "Go for it."

Bending over, Amir slammed his arms against his backside.

But the zip tie failed to break. Amir tried again. Still it held.

"Is this the same as the other zip ties?" asked Amir.

Steve nodded.

"Have another go," urged Connor. "You just need to get the right angle."

Amir kept thumping away, but the zip tie refused to snap. Becoming more and more frustrated with each attempt, Amir waddled around the restaurant's private dining room, grunting, his arms flapping wildly.

"He's like a chicken doing a break-dance!" joked Richie.

Everyone at the table collapsed into fits of laughter as Amir stumbled into a chair and fell over.

Steve glanced across at Colonel Black, unable to suppress a grin. "We should make this a regular party game!"

3

"So whose idea was it to kidnap me?" asked Connor, eventually cutting Amir's zip tie for him.

"Mine," said Jason, raising his glass of Coke in salute.

Connor should have guessed. It was typical of his Aussie rival's sense of humor. "Couldn't you have just ordered me a taxi?"

Jason responded with a mischievous grin. "Wouldn't have been half as much fun."

Amir plonked himself down at the table beside Connor. Studying the menu intently to hide his embarrassment, he whispered, "It's harder than it looks."

Connor nodded in sympathy. "Let's just hope you're not kidnapped with zip ties on the mission, eh?"

"Yeah, your Principal might actually die from laughter before being rescued!" chortled Richie.

Amir sank lower in his chair. His slick black hair flopped forward, covering his dark brown eyes but not hiding his dismay. Connor glared at Richie, whose cutting Irish wit had fallen far from the mark this time. Richie shrugged an apology, but it was a little late for that.

Connor patted his friend on the shoulder. "Don't worry. You'll be fine."

"Easy for you to say," muttered Amir. "You've already earned your gold wings." He indicated the gleaming badge pinned on Connor's T-shirt: a winged shield with the silhouette of a bodyguard at its center. "I still haven't proved myself."

Ever since joining Guardian the previous year, Connor knew his friend had been desperate for the colonel to select him to lead a mission. Now Amir was just three weeks from his first solo assignment protecting a young Bollywood film star, and his nerves were starting to show.

"Don't you remember how nervous I was before my first assignment?" said Connor. "I barely slept for a week. And I'd only just completed basic training. You have the benefit of almost a year of instruction, as well as learning from *all* my mistakes!"

Amir managed a strained smile. "Doesn't make it any easier."

"From my experience, it isn't ever easy."

"But what if I fail? Like I just did with the zip ties. Or I freeze at the moment of an attack?"

"You won't," reassured Connor. "Trust me, every bodyguard

worries about such things. But I promise you, your training *will* kick in. You will react. Besides, I'll be back at HQ providing you support, instead of the other way around."

Amir swallowed hard and nodded. "Thanks. It's good to know you'll be there for me."

"Okay, birthday boy," interrupted Charley, "what would you like?"

Connor turned to Charley, who was sitting next to him. She looked stunning in a glittering silver top, her long blond hair braided into a golden plait and a touch of makeup highlighting her sky-blue eyes. It took a few seconds for Connor to become aware of the waitress standing behind her, patiently waiting for his order.

"I can come back to you if you need more time," said the waitress, smiling.

"No, it's all right," replied Connor, hurriedly scanning the menu and hoping Charley hadn't noticed him staring at her. He asked for a large steak with extra fries. The adrenaline rush of the fake kidnapping had given him a serious appetite.

"So, are you heading home to see your family?" Charley asked after placing her own order.

Connor nodded. "The colonel's given me leave at the end of the month."

Charley studied his face, surprised to see a frown. "Aren't you excited to be going?"

He sighed quietly and, lowering his voice, confessed, "Yes, it's just . . . I'm worried about how my mum will be. Last time she was so weak."

Charley's hand touched his arm. "Look, if it would help, I can come with you."

Connor hesitated. "Thanks, but I don't want to put you out."

"It's not a problem," she insisted. "Besides, I could use a change of scenery. I'm getting cabin fever being cooped up at HQ. California girls aren't suited to long winters stuck in Wales."

Connor smiled. He had to admit it would be good to have her company on the long train trip. And at least he could satisfy his mother's curiosity about his friends at his "private boarding school."

"Okay, that would be great—" A large box was thrust between him and Charley.

"Present time!" Ling announced excitedly.

Connor dutifully unwrapped the gift and laughed at what was inside.

"To replace the one I broke," said Ling with a grin as Connor lifted out the padded headguard. Earlier that month he'd been sparring with Ling and she'd executed a devastating jumping ax-kick on him. The blow had split his old headguard in two, as well as making him lose the match.

"I'm just glad you didn't crack my skull open," said Connor, admiring the new full-face guard with shock-suppression gel for maximum protection. "That would've been a lot harder to replace."

"Oh, I don't know," said Ling. "I saw some soccer balls about the size of your head. Plant one of those atop your neck and I'd have something else to kick."

"Just wait till the next time we spar—I'll kick *you* through the goal posts!" Connor shot back. With the score even at four bouts each, they both knew their next sparring match would be hard fought. He'd even heard rumors that the instructors were laying bets on who would win.

Jason tossed Connor a poorly wrapped gift. "Hope it fits."

The packaging split open on landing to reveal a garish yellow T-shirt with a picture of a koala with sharpened teeth and the warning *Beware Drop Bears!* The design was a painful reminder of the time Connor had fallen for Jason's hoax about killer koalas on his last mission. Holding the T-shirt against himself for size, Connor couldn't help but smile.

"Is it bulletproof?" he asked.

"Nah," said Jason in his Aussie twang. "But it's guaranteed to repel drop bears!"

"Like the cologne you wear to repel girls, then?" quipped Richie, causing the others to laugh.

Jason snarled. "Hey, my cologne works just fine," he said, putting an arm around Ling.

Ling smiled sweetly before elbowing him hard in the ribs.

Jason doubled over in pain. *"Oof!* Talk about tough love,"
he wheezed.

While Jason recovered from Ling's "affectionate" elbow
strike, Connor unwrapped his other gifts. Marc had bought
him a designer shirt from Paris. Richie had given him the latest Assassin's Creed game, and last but not least was a joint
gift from Amir and Charley.

"I hope you like it," said Charley, biting her lower lip
anxiously as she handed him a small box. "Amir helped
choose it."

Connor pulled off the lid. Inside was a G-Shock Range-
man watch.

Amir leaned over, eager to show him the watch's features.
"It's solar powered with multiband six atomic timekeeping,
an auto-LED super illuminator, a triple sensor and a digital compass. But most important for you, it's waterproof and
shock resistant. Engineered to stand up to the most gruel-
ing conditions imaginable. Basically, this is one gadget you
won't be able to break."

"Thanks, guys . . . It's awesome," said Connor, slipping the
watch on and holding up his wrist for the others to admire it.

"An ideal gift for a bodyguard," remarked Colonel Black
with a nod of approval. "An accurate timepiece is essential
on missions. But there's one final present."

He slid a set of car keys down the glass table to Connor. Everyone's jaws dropped open in shock.

"You're giving him a *car*!" exclaimed Jason.

"Driving lessons, to be exact," replied Jody. "The car is for all Alpha team to use."

Connor picked up the keys, staring at them in astonishment. "But I'm *way* too young to drive."

Colonel Black shook his head. "In a dangerous situation, no bodyguard's too young."

4

"The heart of Africa will *beat* again!" exclaimed Michel Feruzi. The Burundian minister for trade and tourism thumped the well-worn wooden conference table with a fleshy fist, the glasses of iced water jingling from his overzealous blow.

"I agree," chimed in Uzair Mossi, the eyes of the finance minister sparkling like the very diamonds they were talking about. "Too long has Burundi been the poor man of this rich continent. If the rumors are true, then this is a turning point for our nation, a—"

President Bagaza held up his hand for silence and waited for his ministers to curb their premature celebrations. He did not share their enthusiasm at the news.

"Angola. Sierra Leone. Liberia. The Congo," he said in his low, solemn tone. "Do their tragic histories not mean anything to you?" He let the ghosts of each country's brutal civil war, fueled by blood diamonds, settle in the minds of his ministers before continuing. "The reported discovery of a diamond field is a reason to both rejoice and despair. After a generation of tribal conflict, our country's peace is fragile at best. We cannot, *must not,* let ourselves be dragged back into civil war."

The ministers exchanged uneasy looks. Although the bloodshed had ended a decade earlier, scars still ran deep, and the tensions between rival Hutu and Tutsi factions bubbled just beneath the surface, even within the government itself.

"The president is right," declared Minister Feruzi, his chair creaking as he settled his ample bulk into the seat. "We've only recently relocated all the Batwa tribes from the expanded Ruvubu National Park. If they learn that there's a diamond field, they'll make a claim over their ancestral lands. We cannot allow one minority tribal group to solely benefit. The whole country must prosper from this discovery."

"That's *if* there are diamonds in the first place," commented the minister for energy and mines. Adrien Rawasa, a thin man with a shaved head, hollow cheeks and rounded spectacles, stood and tapped a faded, out-of-date geological map of Burundi on the whitewashed wall.

"As you're well aware, Mr. President, our mining sector is still in its infancy. We have substantial deposits of nickel, cobalt and copper that can only be exploited with the help of foreign investors. We even have some seams of gold and uranium. But we're not blessed—or cursed, as you may see it—with the same bounty of natural resources as our neighbors. The land within the national park isn't typical of the geology in which diamonds are found. The rumor might well have started from stones illegally smuggled across the border from the Congo or Rwanda."

"But is it conceivable there *could* be diamonds in the park?" questioned President Bagaza.

Minister Rawasa sucked at his lower lip as he studied the map. "Well ... let's just say it's not impossible."

"Then we must tread very carefully. Minister Feruzi, close off the national park and order the rangers to begin a sector-by-sector search. I want confirmation that the diamond field is real before we start raising hopes and making plans. Tell the rangers they're looking for poachers but to report anything else unusual. The last thing we need is a false diamond rush."

"Should I delay the French diplomat's visit?" asked Minister Feruzi.

President Bagaza repeatedly clicked the top of his ballpoint pen, considering the proposal for a moment. "No. Not after the millions France has invested in the conservation program. If we don't show them progress, they'll cut off all our international aid. And we can't afford to lose such funding." He gave everyone at the table a meaningful look. "In the meantime, this news isn't to go any farther than this room. Understood?"

His ministers nodded obediently. But President Bagaza knew it was a futile request. He trusted no one on his cabinet to keep a secret. And if his government ministers had heard about the diamonds, then there was no doubt that other, more dangerous individuals would know too. Diamonds lured corrupt men like wasps to a jam jar.

5

"ATTACK FRONT!" shouted Jody as a car sped out of a side street and screeched to a halt in the middle of the road.

Connor slammed on the brakes. Jody braced herself in the passenger seat, while in the back Charley and Marc were flung forward, saved only by their seat belts. Crunching gears, Connor battled to find reverse. He'd been driving only three weeks, and the pressure of an ambush was seriously testing his new skills.

"*Come on,*" he muttered in frustration as the attackers jumped out of their vehicle.

"Maybe you should learn to drive in America?" Charley suggested with a wry smile.

"What difference would *that* make?" he said, rattling the gearshift furiously.

"All our cars are automatic!"

Finally Connor managed to engage reverse, looked over his shoulder and accelerated away hard. The engine whined in protest as the tachometer maxed out. Gripping the steering wheel tightly, Connor fought to maintain a straight line and stay on the road. Driving fast in reverse was judged extremely dangerous—one tiny misjudgment and he could send the car into a fatal spinout.

By now their attackers had begun firing at them. Connor's car was going flat out, but reverse gear wasn't anywhere near fast enough to escape the ambush. To do so, he had to change direction. Adrenaline pumping, he took his foot off the accelerator, wrenched the steering wheel hard to the right and applied the hand brake, all at the same time. His car went into a tire-screeching 180-degree pivot and came to a tight stop. Releasing the hand brake, he floored the accelerator pedal and they shot off again, speeding away from the kill zone.

Behind him, Connor heard Marc whistle in relief and Charley whisper, "That's one hell of a roller-coaster ride!"

"Well done, Connor. Aside from the poor gear change, that was a textbook J-turn," Jody commended, checking off another box on her clipboard.

Connor eased off the accelerator, pleased to have passed the first stage. As he continued down the road, he routinely checked his rearview mirror in case the ambushers decided to pursue them. After three weeks of intensive lessons, he and the rest of Alpha team had completed their basic driving test and were on to advanced evasive driving skills. They'd been taught how to execute a sharp 180-degree bootlegger's turn, drive safely at high speed, control a skid, push an immobilized vehicle out of the kill zone, and even force another car off the road in a pursuit. Now it was time to put their newly acquired skills to the test.

Jody had explained that car travel was inherently dangerous. Compared with the security in place at a VIP's home or a school, a vehicle was a mobile target. At these times, the Principal was at their most vulnerable to attack or kidnap attempts. This was why each member of Alpha team had to be able to drive with confidence and at high speeds. One never knew when they might have to take charge of a vehicle in an emergency.

"Watch out!" cried Marc, just as Connor turned a corner.

Up ahead two cars were parked nose to nose across the street, blocking Connor's way. There wasn't enough distance to execute a bootlegger's turn. So this time, Connor didn't stop. He drove straight at the roadblock. He knew his aim would be critical. It had to be the front wheels of the blockading cars; otherwise it would be impossible to ram them out of the way. The cars' front-wheel arches were solid and would give him the resistance he needed, as well as the angle of force to pivot the vehicles aside.

When he was sixty feet away, Connor purposely slowed down, dropped into first gear, then accelerated hard. He had to hit the roadblock at just the right speed. Too slow and he'd get stuck. Too fast and he'd damage his own car.

"Brace yourselves!" he warned.

There was a gut-wrenching crunch as they struck the blockade. The impact was jarring, but not devastating enough to disable his own vehicle. In preparation for the training exercise, the car's airbags had been disarmed so the collision didn't trigger their inflation and cut the engine.

As he pushed on through the blockade, Connor heard another horrible *scrunching* sound and went to brake.

"Don't stop," urged Charley.

Connor kept his foot firmly on the accelerator, but the scraping between the cars was like fingernails being clawed down a chalkboard. Then, with a final *screech*, they were beyond the roadblock.

Charley looked back out of the rear window. "Don't worry, it was just your front bumper falling off!" she said, keeping her voice light and breezy.

Grimacing, Connor prayed Jody wouldn't penalize him for such an error. He'd been warned about the danger of getting tangled up with another vehicle. Driving on, he tried to sneak a glance at Jody's test sheet just as a masked man leaped into the road. On instinct, Connor braked, stopping a couple of feet short of hitting him. Unfazed, the attacker raised his gun and fired. A red paintball exploded on the windshield, directly in line with Connor's head.

"Test over," declared Jody.

The gunman walked up to the driver's side and tapped on the glass. Connor wound down the window. Bending down, the gunman removed his mask.

"Better luck next time," said Bugsy as Jody put a cross through the last box on her clipboard. "Consider us even for kicking me in the jaw!"

With a sinking heart, Connor flicked on the windshield wipers and washed off the glob of dripping paint. Turning the car around, he headed back to the starting point—the forecourt of the abandoned business park commandeered for the exercise. He stopped beside Amir, Ling, Jason and Richie, huddled in a group, all wrapped up in thick puffer jackets against the winter chill.

Stepping out of the car, Connor noticed Marc clasping his right side as if in pain. "Are you all right?" he asked.

"Fine," replied Marc, waving him away. "The seat belt must have caught me when you did the emergency stop. Don't worry about it."

"How did the test go?" asked Amir, his breath puffing out in small white clouds in the cold air.

Connor responded with a half-hearted smile.

"Not good, by the looks of it," remarked Richie, examining the beat-up fender. "He's trashed our car!"

"Sorry," Connor mumbled. "I must have gotten tangled up."

Jody inspected the damage herself. "It's mostly cosmetic. The good thing was you didn't stop and the car wasn't disabled." She stood and addressed all of Alpha team. "The number one rule in an ambush situation is to *always keep moving*." Making another mark on her clipboard, she glanced over at Connor. "Shame you didn't do that on the final stage of the exercise."

"But I'd have run Bugsy over," protested Connor.

"It was *only* Bugsy," she replied, the corner of her mouth curling up in a wry smile. "Seriously, in such a situation you shouldn't hesitate to use your vehicle as a weapon to attack a threat head-on."

"But you could kill someone!" said Amir.

"That's their decision. If there's an armed attacker in front of your car, you drive into, around or over that attacker. No hesitation. And when you drive directly at the enemy, their self-preservation instincts kick in. This affects their ability to shoot straight, as well as shifting their focus from killing you to not getting hit themselves. Either way, the threat is neutralized or escape achieved."

"So I've failed the test, then?" said Connor, glumly looking at the smear of red paint still visible on the windshield.

"You're technically dead," Jody admitted. Then she gave him an encouraging wink. "However, your overall score was seventy-eight percent. A solid pass."

Ling punched Connor on the arm. "Slick driving, hotshot! Almost as good as Mad Max here." She nodded at Jason. "In his test, he nearly mowed Bugsy down."

"At least I didn't get shot," Jason said defensively.

"But you almost lost control of the car," cautioned Jody. "That's why a vehicle is probably the deadliest weapon you'll have at your disposal. And like any other weapon, if it's handled incorrectly, you can kill yourself, and your friends, with it. But if you handle it correctly, you can save lives."

6

"Connor, you're home!" his mom called out brightly as he and Charley were dropped off by the taxi. She came down the path to greet them. But as she approached the rickety gate of their East London town house, she suddenly lost her footing. Her walking stick went out from under her, and she toppled over. Only Connor's fast reactions saved his mom from a nasty fall. He leaped forward, catching her in his arms.

"Whoops," she said with an embarrassed glance up at him. "Must have slipped on some ice."

Connor nodded, accepting her excuse without argument. However, as cold as the winter weather was, he couldn't see any ice. As he helped her stand, he noticed a distinct tremor in his mom's body. Although it might have been the shock of the fall, he suspected it was another symptom of her multiple sclerosis. She looked more fragile than ever, as if the slightest breeze might blow her away like a leaf. Her cheeks were more sunken, and the constant pain she suffered from seemed to have etched permanent wrinkles at the corners of her eyes. Connor felt tears welling up in his own and fought against them. It was tragically apparent to him that the disease had strengthened its grip on his mom and was slowly yet surely squeezing the mobility from her frail body.

But her smile remained defiant, and her embrace was powerful with love. As he returned her hug, glad for the chance to blink away his tears, she seemed to take strength from his presence; when he pulled away, her face had visibly brightened, as if a shadow had been lifted.

"It's so good to see you," she said, kissing his cheek. Then she looked past him to Charley, only a flicker of surprise passing across her face before she offered a heartfelt greeting. "You must be Charley. Welcome! Sorry about the dramatic reception."

"Don't worry, Mrs. Reeves," replied Charley, entering the front yard. "I'm just pleased to meet you. Connor's talked about you a lot."

"Really?" said his mom, taking her walking stick from her son but declining his offer of support. "Well, I hope it was all good. Now, you both must be tired from your journey. Come in before we all freeze to death."

They followed her through the front door, where Connor noticed a newly installed ramp and a folded-up wheelchair in the hallway. His mom's deteriorating condition was worse than he'd feared.

In the living room his gran was waiting by the fireside. The coals in the grate glowed red, giving off a steady warmth and flickering light that Connor always associated with being home.

"How's my big man?" asked his gran, rising slowly from her armchair, as old and worn as she was.

"Fine, Gran. And you?"

"As fit as a fiddle and . . ."

"As right as rain," Connor finished for her.

"Hey, you cheeky scamp! That's my line." She laughed, pulling him into a hug. "Now, who's the beauty behind you?"

Stepping aside, Connor introduced Charley, who handed his gran a gift box of fine teas.

"Connor told me you like Earl Grey," she explained.

"Why, that's very thoughtful of you," his gran replied, admiring the fancy label on the box. Connor could tell his gran had instantly warmed to Charley by the way she gently patted her hand in thanks. "Make yourself at home, Charley, while Connor and I get some tea and cookies."

Connor dutifully followed his gran into the kitchen, leaving Charley with his mom. He briefly looked back to check that Charley was all right, but they were already chatting happily.

"Where's Sally?" Connor asked, referring to the live-in caretaker that the Guardian organization provided in return for his services as a bodyguard.

"Oh, we've given her the afternoon off since you're here," explained his gran, flicking on the kettle and taking out her best china from a cupboard.

"Is that wise?" asked Connor, his eyes drawn to the wheel-chair in the hall. "Mum seems rather ... weak."

His gran paused in making the tea. With a heavy sigh, she answered, "Your mum's having a relapse. She won't admit how much she's suffering. That's why she insisted on greeting you at the gate, despite my protests. She wanted to prove to you she's doing well. Didn't want you worrying at school."

Connor glanced into the living room, where his mom now sat by the fire, the tremor in her hands still visible. Despite everything he was doing to provide their live-in care, he still felt powerless to help her where it mattered most. He wished he could somehow *protect* her from the disease, rather than merely help ease her suffering.

His gran saw the anguish in his face. "Don't worry, my love. Your mum's keeping up her spirits. And Sally's a god-send. I honestly don't know how we'd cope without her help. Anyway, your Charley seems a lovely girl," his gran remarked, changing topics as she popped four Earl Grey teabags into the pot and poured in hot water. "So what's the story with you two?"

"We're just friends," replied Connor, realizing where this was leading.

Gran gave him a look.

"No, really," insisted Connor.

"I believe you," she said with a knowing smile as she arranged some cookies on a plate. "But I hope you don't mind me saying, she seems an unusual choice of student to be in a 'school' like yours."

Unlike his mom, Connor's gran knew the truth about the "private boarding school" he attended. Although Colonel Black had sworn him to secrecy because the Guardian organization relied on its covert status to function effectively, Connor had realized that his gran was too sharp-witted to be fooled. She'd have seen straight through any lies. So, trusting his gran implicitly, he'd told her about the deal—the scholarship program set up by Guardian to fund their care and his education in exchange for becoming a bodyguard. She hadn't liked the proposal one bit, yet was a realist when it came to their family's desperate situation. She'd also recognized his late father's steely determination in him—a determination that had made his father the best of the best: a soldier in the Special Air Service. So, although she hadn't given her full blessing, she'd accepted his decision to join.

From the living room, Connor heard Charley laugh at something his mom said and just hoped his mom wasn't telling any embarrassing stories about him as a boy.

"So what happened to Charley?" pressed his gran, picking

up the tea tray. She directed her gaze to the wheelchair Charley sat in.

Connor barely noticed it anymore. Charley had made clear, both in words and action, that her chair did not define her. "I don't know exactly," he replied. "She's never told me. It happened before I joined, on an assignment."

His gran almost dropped the tray, the cups clattering and the pot splashing steaming tea on the linoleum floor. "On an *assignment*!"

Unable to meet his gran's hard stare, Connor grabbed a cloth from the sink to wipe up the mess.

Putting the tray down on the countertop, his gran looked thoughtfully out the kitchen window. "It doesn't seem right that this colonel of yours is allowed to recruit young people for such a dangerous job. Sacrificing their futures to protect others." She shook her head in sad disbelief. "What is the world coming to when an organization like this is even *needed*?"

Connor's gran turned back to him, her expression set. "I'm no longer comfortable with this Guardian arrangement. Not anymore."

"But, Gran, I can assure you, the risks are minimal," insisted Connor. "We're very well trained and plan for all eventualities."

"Obviously not *all* eventualities," retorted his gran, directing her gaze to Charley in the living room. "I want you to quit. Before something terrible happens to you."

"But I can't," argued Connor. "It pays for all the care you and Mum need."

"I know . . . I know," said his gran, taking a step toward him and cupping his face between her palms, just like she used to when he was a little boy. She studied it with a pained expression of love and deep concern. "There's so much of your father in you. And of course I realize this organization pays for our care. But at what cost exactly?"

7

"You two took your time," remarked his mom, breaking away from her conversation with Charley as Connor and his gran came back into the living room. "We thought you must have been devouring all the cookies!"

"No, dear, I just spilled some tea on the floor," Gran explained, settling into her armchair.

"But it's all cleared up now, isn't it, Gran?" said Connor as he placed the tray on a side table.

In return, she offered him a tight-lipped smile. After much persuasion, he'd managed to convince her that he should continue being a bodyguard, at least for the time being. He'd assured her that he wasn't assigned to the next mission so would be safe back at HQ. His gran had relented, albeit reluctantly, but only on the condition they'd discuss the issue again at the Easter break. She was adamant that he shouldn't be risking his own life to pay for their care. Connor, however, felt differently. With his father dead, he had a responsibility to provide for his family, especially when their needs were so great—even if there were risks.

Connor certainly wasn't blind to the dangers. He'd faced deadly situations on both his missions so far. But his training, and admittedly some luck, had helped him to survive. Besides, he didn't *want* to leave Guardian. The intensity of the training and the pressure of being on a mission had forged an invisible bond between the members of Alpha team. They were now his closest and most trusted friends. He didn't want to break that bond, especially with Charley.

"I like your hairstyle in this photo," said Charley, holding up a picture of him at five years old. He was wearing just a pair of shorts and held an ice pop in one hand. His green-blue eyes were bright with delight, and his dark brown hair was shaped into a humiliating bowl cut, a far cry from the spiky style he now sported.

Connor squirmed with embarrassment when he realized his mom had pulled out the family album. "Mum! That's *not* cool."

"But it's a mother's prerogative to embarrass her son," she said, sharing a mischievous wink with Charley. "In fact, I was thinking of telling Charley about the time you put your underpants on your head and—"

"No!" cut in Connor, mortified.

Charley suppressed a giggle and pointed to another

photo of him dressed as Superman. "You were so cute as a little boy. What happened to you?" she teased.

"I decided to keep my alter ego hidden," replied Connor, retrieving the family album from her and returning it to its rightful place on the shelf. He gave Charley an imploring look. "Please don't tell anyone back at school."

"Too late." She held up her smartphone. "I've shared it online."

Connor's jaw dropped in dismay. "You're not serious, are you?"

Charley and his mom burst into laughter.

"Would I do something like that?" Charley replied with an impish curl of her lips. "Although I might save a copy, just in case I need to keep you in line."

Hoping to move swiftly on from the cringe-worthy photos, Connor poured out the tea and handed everyone a cup.

"Shall we give Connor his birthday present now?" his gran suggested as he sat down beside his mom on the sofa.

Nodding, his mom produced a package from behind a cushion.

Connor unwrapped the gift to reveal a black knitted sweater.

"Thanks . . . It's lovely," he said, trying to sound enthusiastic.

"To keep you warm in the Brecons," explained his gran. "I resisted the urge to knit a snowman on the front. I thought that wouldn't be very hip for school."

"You're absolutely right," agreed Connor.

"Why not try it on?" encouraged his mom.

Connor unfolded the sweater, and that's when he discovered the other gifts: a medal embossed with an American eagle and a survival knife.

"These were my dad's!" he exclaimed breathlessly. Connor swallowed hard as he found himself overcome with emotion. After his father's death, his mom had kept such things in a memory box, along with photos and other personal items that defined his father.

"Well, they're yours now," declared his mom with a bittersweet smile. "I've checked with your school, and there's no problem taking the knife back with you. In fact, your head teacher, Mr. Black, positively encouraged it." She raised an eyebrow to express her surprise. "I don't know if I ever told you, but that medal was awarded posthumously to your father for saving a US ambassador's life."

Connor nodded. "Yeah, he's now the president of the United States," he said without thinking.

"How do *you* know that?" exclaimed his mom. "I don't think I was even told the ambassador's name."

Connor immediately tried to backtrack. He knew this fact only because, on his first assignment to protect the US president's daughter, he'd met the man himself, who had told him about his father's heroic sacrifice. "I . . . must have read it in a newspaper."

"Would you like some more tea, Mrs. Reeves?" asked Charley, intervening before his mom could interrogate him further. Connor knew that if she discovered his secret life as a bodyguard, it would bring an end to everything, however much she was in need of proper care. And although he didn't like deceiving her, in this case, the ends justified the lie.

"Um . . . yes, please," replied his mom, holding out her cup with a tremulous hand.

While the others drank their tea and Charley led the conversation away from US presidents, Connor, avoiding his mom's quizzical gaze, examined his father's survival knife. The handle was made of rosewood, well oiled and smooth to the touch. When he slid the blade out of its leather sheath, he could see that it was razor sharp and in perfect condition. As he held the knife in one hand and the medal in the other, memories of his father came flooding back, in particular those of their camping trips together—*cutting down branches and making a bivouac shelter, using a flint and steel to start a campfire, skinning a rabbit and cooking it over the open flames, lying beneath the night sky and learning how to navigate by the stars . . .*

"Would you help me clear away, Charley?" said his gran quietly.

"Sure," replied Charley, moving the tea tray onto her lap.

When the two of them had left the living room, Connor's mom edged closer on the sofa and put her arm around him.

Connor let himself be drawn into her comfort, allowing the grief for his dead father to flow out.

Eventually, wiping his eyes with the back of his hand, Connor looked up. "Thanks, Mum," he said, hugging her. "This is the best present possible."

"I'm glad you like them," she said, kissing him on the forehead. Then lowering her voice and glancing toward the kitchen, she asked, "So is this the girl who's been distracting you from your schoolwork?"

Connor felt his cheeks flush. "She's just a friend," he insisted.

"Well, she's lovely." His mom tousled his hair affectionately. "And you're such a good boy. Always looking out for others." Her expression became solemn again. "Now, please don't get me wrong when I say this, but do you really need to burden yourself further?"

"I'm not sure I understand," said Connor.

His mom sighed softly, and her gaze drifted to the kitchen and Charley in her wheelchair. "You've got enough on your plate with me and Gran. Should you really be taking on Charley's needs as well?"

Connor looked toward the kitchen and saw his gran fumble with a teacup, but Charley caught it in midair, her reflexes as sharp as ever.

Connor smiled to himself. "Charley doesn't need *me* to look after her," he assured his mom. "She can more than handle herself, in any situation."

"Well, *that* I can believe," said his mom, giving him a final inquisitive look but taking it no further. "I was only thinking of you. Forget I ever mentioned it. If the truth be told, I should take my inspiration from Charley's attitude to life's daily challenges . . ."

Connor became aware that his mom's tremors were getting worse. But it wasn't her MS this time. He could see she was on the verge of tears. At that very moment Charley and his gran reentered the living room with a large chocolate birthday cake decorated with fifteen candles. His mom immediately rallied and joined in singing "Happy Birthday" as the cake was placed before him on the table.

"Don't forget to make a wish," urged Charley when he leaned forward to blow out the candles.

Closing his eyes, Connor had only one wish in the world.

8

"Is this where you found the diamond?" demanded General Pascal, surveying the hidden valley. Thick vegetation cloaked the steep sides, and a primeval mist hung ghost-like in the dawn air, seemingly undisturbed for millennia. A wide, shallow river snaked its way over rocks and through gullies, twisting downhill toward a waterfall that joined the Ruvubu River in the distance. To the west was a craggy peak, atop which stood a single acacia tree.

No Mercy recognized the peak from his former life, a life erased since his abduction and forced conscription into the ANL, the Armée Nationale de la Liberté. The peak was called Dead Man's Hill. An ancient sacrificial site. No one from the villages ventured near for fear of evil spirits and man-eating leopards. It was little wonder this valley had lain undisturbed for so long—until now. No Mercy kicked at the mud and stones with his bare feet. Who would have imagined there were diamonds here? They all looked like worthless rocks to him.

General Pascal turned impatiently to a thin, gaunt-faced man at his side. Tongue-tied, the prisoner stared up at him with round, fearful eyes.

"Answer the general!" ordered Blaze, striking the man so hard across the jaw that the prisoner dropped to his knees, spitting blood.

A tooth fell from the poor man's mouth, and he reached with a trembling hand to pick it back up. Blaze stepped on the man's fingers, crushing them against the rocks.

"Another for my collection," Blaze remarked, taking the tooth for himself. The general's right-hand man had a reputation for cruelty. Never seen without his mirrored aviator sunglasses or the fearsome machete that hung from his hip, he wore an army-green T-shirt, black combat pants and matching boots. He kept his head shaved, and around his neck hung a beaded necklace, which on closer inspection was made up of human teeth.

Beaten into submission, the prisoner pointed to a sandy bank on the bend of the river. "Right here," he spluttered through a mouthful of blood. "I found the diamond right here."

General Pascal pulled a brand-new Glock 17 from his hip

holster and pressed the barrel against the man's temple. "You wouldn't lie to me, would you?"

The man shook his head, his whole body trembling in terror. "No, General! I swear!"

"Good," said General Pascal, smiling at him as he squeezed the trigger.

The gunshot echoed around the valley, startling birds from treetops and sending monkeys into a shrieking panic. The man flopped lifeless into the river, his blood mixing with the water and turning it pale pink. Pink as a rare diamond.

A child soldier, wearing combat fatigues and a black bandana with *Dredd* emblazoned across the brow, prodded the bleeding corpse with a toe.

"Why you kill him?" he questioned the general, more bemused than shocked.

General Pascal sneered at the boy as if the answer was obvious. "He tried to steal *my* diamonds. This land belongs to me now." He planted a foot on the dead man's back and declared, "We'll start digging here."

No Mercy jerked the barrel of his gleaming AK-47 at the group of prisoners they'd rounded up from a distant village. Without needing to be told twice, the men picked up their shovels and sieves and set to work panning for diamonds. No Mercy smirked at their doglike obedience.

"I don't want anyone else knowing where this diamond field is," announced the general. He pointed to a number of potential access points around the secluded valley. "Blaze, set up guards there, there and there. Kill anyone who attempts to enter or leave this valley."

9

Connor stifled a yawn as he tapped away on the keyboard in the operations room at Guardian HQ. Equipped with state-of-the-art computers, satellite phones and HD flat-screen displays streaming live news feeds and the latest world security updates, the operations room was the hub of Alpha team's activities. Every piece of intelligence, every threat assessment and every mission profile was stored here. All security decisions and operational orders were issued from this room.

Connor was at the end of his shift and completing the daily occurrence log. Dull but essential work. Each shift leader had to record everything that occurred during an assignment, whether routine or out of the ordinary. That meant every phone call, every communication, every incident, every change in plan. *Any* occurrence, no matter how seemingly insignificant—from the driver's name of a delivery company to the scheduled maintenance of an air-conditioning unit to the details of a vehicle parked outside a Principal's house. Such mundane information, as Bugsy their surveillance tutor had repeatedly stressed, could become crucial later in an operation—when the driver of the delivery company became a suspect, or a bugging device was detected in a vent, or the same vehicle was spotted in another location.

But as important as his work was, Connor simply couldn't get excited about it. After a week stationed at HQ supporting Amir on his first mission, Connor was yearning for the challenge of an assignment himself. Nothing compared with the "buzz" and heightened perception that came from protecting a Principal in the field. Colors seemed brighter, sounds sharper and sensations stronger. He could now understand what his father meant when he'd referred to the "combat high" that soldiers experienced during battle. Connor experienced a similar "protection high."

Finishing the log entry, Connor leaned back in his chair and stretched his limbs. He felt his father's knife pressing against his hip, as if spurring him to go on another mission. He'd originally become a bodyguard not just to provide care for his family but to follow in his father's footsteps and discover more about the man he'd barely known—an SAS operative on the Special Projects Team, responsible for counterterrorism and VIP close protection, a man who'd saved not only a future president's life but also Colonel Black's. And now, after two successful missions, Connor felt as if he was walking side by side with his father. He'd come to appreciate why his father had dedicated himself to protecting others—that sense of pride and purpose in keeping someone safe. But it was only on an assignment that he felt so close to him. Back at HQ, his father seemed to withdraw into nothing but the picture Connor kept of him on his key fob.

Despite the lack of thrills that came with being stuck at HQ, Connor couldn't deny there were some benefits. He got the chance to hang out with Charley and the rest of Alpha team. He could keep up his kickboxing training, critical for his forthcoming match with Ling. He even had the time to read and watch some TV. That said, he and the others wouldn't be getting any free time over the coming week or so. Alpha team had been tasked with running two assignments simultaneously—Operation Hawk-Eye, which Amir was already on, and Operation Lionheart, which Marc was due to commence in just under twenty-four hours.

Connor glanced over to the briefing room, where Marc, Jason, Ling and Charley were finalizing the op-orders. Marc had been assigned to protect a French diplomat's family on safari in Africa. It sounded like a dream assignment to Connor.

Yet Marc didn't appear too thrilled at the prospect. A sheen of sweat glistened on his forehead, and his complexion was rather pale. Suddenly Marc made a retching sound, clamped a hand to his mouth and ran from the room.

Jason looked around at the others in bewilderment. "I know Marc gets the jitters before a mission, but I've never seen him *that* bad."

Connor rose from his seat, intending to see if Marc was all right, but at that moment his computer monitor flashed and an alert sounded, notifying him of an incoming video call. Connor clicked Accept and Amir's face popped up on the screen.

"You're not due to report in for another hour," said Connor. "Everything okay?"

But he could tell from Amir's expression that things were far from right.

"Is anyone else with you?" Amir asked.

Connor looked across to the briefing room, then shook his head. "They're all dealing with Marc at the moment. Seems like he's having a panic attack."

"He's not the only one," replied Amir, his voice strained.

Connor leaned closer to the screen, his concern growing. "What's happened?"

Amir took a deep breath. "I'm not like you, Connor … I'm no kickboxing champion. I don't have a fighter's natural reflexes."

Connor could see his friend was trembling. "Just tell me what's going on."

"We were in a crowd . . . There was a man. I thought he had a grenade . . . I froze. I didn't do anything to protect my Principal—didn't even shout a warning . . ." Amir lapsed into silence, an expression of deep shame on his face.

"Is the Principal okay?" asked Connor.

Amir nodded, but still didn't raise his eyes to the camera. "Yes, fine. The grenade turned out to be an egg!" He shrugged with embarrassment. "But what if it hadn't been—"

"Amir, calm down," interrupted Connor. "It sounds to me like first-operation nerves. You're bound not to react instantaneously, especially when it's the first *real* threat you've encountered. The main thing is your Principal is alive and unharmed."

"Sort of," admitted Amir. "The egg ruined his clothes." He sighed heavily and stared glumly down at his lap. "I don't think I'm cut out for this guardian work. I'm just a slum boy who got lucky. I'm a fake!"

"Don't you dare say that," replied Connor. "Listen, Amir, if you can survive a slum upbringing, get yourself out and provide for your family back in India, then you're more than capable of protecting someone."

Amir had once confided in him about his past. He was the sixth son of a migrant worker from a slum on the outskirts of Delhi. He'd been working as a rag picker, earning a few rupees a month to help stave off his family's hunger, when Colonel Black had discovered him through an unusual "hole-in-the-wall" experiment. An Indian IT company had installed a computer in a concrete wall facing the slum. Without any training or help, Amir and some other slum children had taught themselves how to use the computer. Within a day, Amir was accessing the Internet and creating folders. After a week he was downloading apps, music files and games. By the second month he was writing his own simple programs. With no formal education, Amir had proven himself a natural with computers. He came to Colonel Black's attention when one day he hacked into the IT company's server—a server that was under the colonel's security control at the time. Recognizing his natural talent for problem solving, Colonel Black sponsored Amir through school and recruited him as a potential guardian.

"Remember what the colonel said: the mind is the best weapon a bodyguard can possess," continued Connor. "And you've got a phenomenal mind. So stay focused and in Code Yellow," he advised, referring to the default alert status for a bodyguard. "Next time you'll spot the threat earlier and be able to avoid turning your Principal into an omelet."

Amir managed a half-hearted laugh. "Thanks, Connor . . . I'm glad I've got you for backup."

"You'll be fine," reassured Connor.

Charley came up behind him as Amir signed off. "Any problems?"

Connor turned around and shook his head. "No, Amir's doing great."

"Good," replied Charley, "because Colonel Black needs to see you and says it's urgent."

10

"Change of plan, Connor," said Colonel Black, seated in his antique red leather chair behind the mahogany desk in his office. On the wall, a wide-screen monitor displayed the news of a terrorist attack in China; another was showing the continued riots in Thailand. "You're to be BG on Operation Lionheart."

"What about Marc?" said Connor, confused by the sudden reassignment.

"Our medical officer says he has acute appendicitis," explained Charley, rolling up beside him. "Marc believed it was just a stomach virus and had been trying to tough it out. Jody's rushing him to the hospital now before his appendix bursts."

Connor recalled how his friend had been clutching his side after the advanced driving test the week before. "Will he be all right?"

"He'll be fine," the colonel said. "But you're to stand in for him. You leave tomorrow."

"But . . ." Connor's feelings were conflicted. He was obviously thrilled at the prospect; yet at the forefront of his mind were Amir and his agreement with his gran. "I'm supposed to be Amir's support."

Colonel Black waved away his concerns. "Charley will cover for you. Besides, it's only for ten days."

"What about Jason? Or Richie?"

The colonel shook his head. "They don't have the necessary vaccinations for travel in Africa. Yellow fever and hepatitis A need to be administered at least two weeks in advance. Thankfully, after your last assignment you're already immunized."

Connor appreciated the fact that the decision was out of his hands. Thinking about it, he supposed a short mission was acceptable. His gran wouldn't even know he was gone, and he'd be back in time for the second phase of Amir's assignment. With his conscience almost clear, Connor began to feel the familiar pre-mission rush of anticipation.

"Charley, brief him on the assignment," Colonel Black instructed.

She spun toward the wall monitors and clicked a remote. The news feeds disappeared and were replaced by a picture of a smiling family of four. "As you already know, Operation

Lionheart is tasked with protecting this French diplomat's family on safari in Africa."

"You do realize I don't speak French, right?" Connor asked.

"Not to worry," Charley replied. "The Barbier family all speak English as a second language. And Bugsy will supply you with a new smartphone with a real-time translation app. He has requested, though, that you try to keep *this* phone intact on this mission."

Connor shrugged. "I'll do my best." On his last assignment, his phone had been destroyed by a bullet, though it had saved his life.

"You'll be the guardian for two Principals: Amber and Henri," continued Charley.

A close-up of a flame-haired girl with green eyes appeared on-screen. Next to her, on the other monitor, was an image of a redheaded boy in a blue-and-white soccer jersey.

"Amber's a year older than you are. She's the top goal shooter on her school's netball team, an impressive climber, and has a passion for photography. Her brother, Henri, is nine. As you can see from the photo, he's into soccer—a fan of the Paris Saint-Germain club—but he suffers badly from asthma, so he can't play the game himself."

"Does Amber have any medical conditions?" Connor asked, making mental notes as Charley ran through the brief.

Charley shook her head. "She once broke her foot after a climbing accident, but there weren't any long-term issues, according to her medical files."

With another click of the remote, detailed profiles of both parents were displayed. On the first screen appeared a man in his fifties with cropped gray hair and glasses; on the second was a glamorous middle-aged woman with high cheekbones and auburn hair.

"Laurent, their father, is a long-serving French diplomat who is responsible for managing aid programs in Central Africa. As would be expected of an diplomat, he is well mannered, well connected and sociable. He's also astute and intelligent, with a master's in politics and economics. From what we can gather, he has no known enemies. His only shortcoming was keeping a mistress, although that appears to be in the past."

Charley indicated the mother. "Cerise is a former fashion editor and now a cultural attaché for the French foreign office. A caring mother and apparently forgiving wife, she now accompanies her husband on his diplomatic and foreign trips. By all accounts, she has good relations with family, friends and business colleagues. Nothing unusual—beyond a love of jewelry and an expensive taste in clothing—has been flagged during our profiling of her."

"So, if the Barbiers don't have any obvious enemies, what's the threat?" asked Connor.

Colonel Black leaned forward on his desk, steepling his fingers. "No *specific* threats have been identified for the family. Hence, it's a Category Three operation and the reason why only one guardian has been assigned to two Principals in this instance. Primarily it's the location that raises security issues."

He nodded to Charley, who brought up a map of Central Africa on-screen.

"Laurent Barbier and his family are visiting Burundi by invitation of President Bagaza," Charley explained, pointing to a small heart-shaped country landlocked between the Democratic Republic of Congo, Rwanda and Tanzania. "The purpose of their trip is to experience the country's soon-to-be-opened national park, one that France has heavily invested in."

She enlarged the map to focus on an expanse of uninhabited land in the nation's northeast. Hemmed in by high mountains on either side and split down the center by a silver seam of a river, the area was identified as Ruvubu National Park.

"You see, Burundi is currently the fourth-poorest country in the world," she continued. "After years of civil war crippling their economy, the government is largely dependent on foreign aid. But with peace finally descending some years back, this country is attempting to rebuild itself. Besides exploiting its natural resources, tourism is seen as a potential major source of income. The security situation has improved in recent years, but the country remains subject to political instability and the threat of violence. It's a young, somewhat fragile peace."

The colonel took over. "There's a delicate power-sharing arrangement in place between Burundi's majority Hutu and minority Tutsi communities. The two sides are still struggling to reconcile after decades of conflict. President Bagaza has been sworn in for a second term, which is positive. But he does have his enemies: mainly leaders of former resistance groups, including the FPB—the Front Patriotique Burundais—and the UCL—the Union des Combattants de la Liberté. So, though unlikely, there's always a chance that things could kick off again. That's why the diplomat himself made the request for our services, to ensure his family is one hundred percent safe."

Charley handed Connor a mini USB flash drive. "The op-order has more detail and background on Burundi's civil war, along with an overview of the current state of the country. Don't get your hopes up. It makes for grim reading. The infrastructure is virtually nonexistent. There's little electricity, and the roads are primarily dirt tracks. For what it's worth, I've included the official number for the police under emergency contacts, although it's unlikely anyone will answer your call. So you'll have to rely on your smartphone to contact us if there are any problems—and your only emergency evacuation option will be a private plane."

Pocketing the mini drive, Connor remarked, "Doesn't sound like much of a vacation destination."

Charley smiled. "Don't worry—I've seen pictures of the safari lodge. Luxury is an understatement. Just as an example, the bedroom suites are glass-fronted with their own sundecks and plunge pools. It looks like *millions* have been spent on this tourist project. And with the president's own security forces on hand, this assignment should be a walk in the park for you."

"Still, don't drop your guard, Connor," said Colonel Black. Reaching into his desk drawer, he pulled out a battered pocket manual. "Here, something for you to read on the plane."

He tossed it to Connor. The green-and-orange cover sported the title *SAS Survival Handbook*.

"Expecting problems?" asked Connor, glancing up at the colonel.

Colonel Black shook his head. "No, but it's always best to be prepared for the worst. Especially in Africa."

11

A crude bamboo barrier forced the aging Land Rover to a sudden halt, its tires kicking up plumes of dust from the single-track road that cut through the bush. Two men in threadbare army fatigues, any official insignia long since faded or else purposely removed, stood guard behind the barricade, their assault rifles trained on the vehicle's sole occupant.

The tallest of the men, a gangly Rwandan with deep-set eyes, approached the driver's side. He made a sign to lower the window. Whether the Rwandan was a legitimate border guard or not, the driver complied with the instruction.

"A little off the tourist trail, aren't you?" said the guard, leaning in and eyeing the interior of the 4×4 with greedy interest.

"The main road was blocked," replied the driver.

The guard snorted skeptically. "Passport," he demanded, thrusting out a hand.

The driver reached into his backpack and produced a navy-blue passport. The guard snatched it from his grasp and flicked it open to the ID page. A photo of a lean-faced man with a pale complexion, ice-gray eyes and a dour expression stared back at him. There were no distinguishing features, but the photo more or less matched the driver's appearance. "Stanley Taylor. Canadian?"

Mr. Gray nodded, the fake passport just one of his many false identities.

Leafing through the pages, the guard discovered a crisp ten-dollar bill tucked into the back. He glanced up. "Bribing an official is a crime in our country."

"What bribe?" replied Mr. Gray evenly. "I just gave you my passport as asked for."

The guard closed the document, palming the ten dollars into his own pocket but not returning the passport. "Come with me," he ordered.

Mr. Gray knew the routine. Ten dollars was hardly enough for the two or more guards stationed at this remote border crossing. They would try to squeeze him for more money. Accepted practice. Which was why he hadn't offered anything larger.

Taking his backpack and car keys, Mr. Gray followed the guard into a small wooden building with a corrugated tin roof. Inside it stank of stale sweat and cigarette smoke. After the glare of the African sun, his eyes took a moment to adjust to the dim interior—the only sources of light were the open doorway and a square hole for a window in the back wall. There was a bucket in one corner, a rusted machete leaning against the near wall and an unlit kerosene lamp hanging from a rotting beam. The only pieces of furniture in the room were a battered wooden desk and a chair in which reclined a potbellied official, his feet propped up and a cigarette lolling from his pudgy lips.

The border guard dropped Mr. Gray's passport onto the desk. The official barely glanced at it.

"The purpose of your visit to Rwanda is?" he asked, the cigarette bobbing up and down, discarding ash on the dirt floor.

"Business," replied Mr. Gray.

"And what business might that be?"

"Wildlife photographer."

The officer's eyes narrowed. "Where's your camera?"

"In my bag."

"Search him," he mumbled, jutting his chin in a command to the guard.

Mr. Gray allowed the man to frisk him. His pockets were turned out and his car keys and a slim black wallet deposited on the desk. The official leaned forward and inspected the wallet as the guard rummaged through the backpack.

"For the record, I note you have one hundred dollars in here," he said.

"Two hundred," Mr. Gray corrected.

"No, one hundred," said the official, extracting five twenty-dollar bills and slipping them into his shirt pocket.

"I must have been mistaken," said Mr. Gray with a thin smile.

The border guard pulled out a DSLR digital camera with telephoto lens and held it up for the official to see.

"As I said, wildlife photographer," repeated Mr. Gray.

At that moment the guard from outside entered the shack. Looking directly at the official, he shook his head once. "Nothing in the vehicle."

Not even attempting to hide his disappointment, the official reluctantly opened a drawer and produced a rubber stamp and ink pad. After a protracted and unnecessary examination of the passport, he inked the stamp and was about to authorize entry when the taller guard fumbled and dropped the camera. It hit the floor, the telephoto lens snapping off and rolling to a stop at the foot of the desk. Concealed within the casing was a large pinkish rock.

Mr. Gray silently cursed the guard's clumsiness. It would likely cost the man his life.

Tutting his disapproval, the official set aside his rubber stamp.

"I can explain," said Mr. Gray, his eyes hardening.

"No need," replied the official, bending down to pick up the precious rock and examining it with avaricious delight. "Arrest him."

The tall guard seized Mr. Gray's arms. But a trained assassin isn't easy to restrain. A single reverse head-butt to the face fractured the guard's nose. A spinning elbow strike to the temple rendered him unconscious. And as he crumpled, a sharp, violent twist to the head snapped his neck.

The other guard went for his gun. Grasping the barrel, Mr. Gray wrenched the weapon up and around, spinning it so fast that the man's finger broke in the trigger guard. A single knife-hand strike to the throat crushed his windpipe, cutting off any cry of pain and suffocating the guard even as he writhed on the floor.

In a wild panic, the official snatched up his machete and swung the fearsome blade at Mr. Gray's head. With lightning reflexes, Mr. Gray ducked and simultaneously pulled at the metal buckle of his belt. It came loose to reveal a hidden blade. Before the official could swing again, the assassin leaped across the desk and drove the sharpened point into the man's throat. The official's eyes bulged in agonized shock. The machete clattered to the ground, the cigarette tumbling from the man's quivering lips. As he bled like a stuck pig, his carotid artery severed, Mr. Gray let the official slump into the dirt at his feet.

In less than ten seconds, the three men were dead.

With disconcerting calmness, Mr. Gray retrieved the diamond plus his passport, backpack, camera, car keys, wallet and money the official had stolen, including the ten-dollar bribe in the border guard's pocket. That done, he took the kerosene lamp from the beam and smashed it on the floor. Oil splattered across the corpses, upon which flies were already settling. Then retrieving the still-smoldering cigarette, Mr. Gray tossed it onto the kerosene, and the bodies went up in flames. When anyone eventually reported the men's deaths, it would be assumed that a rogue band of militia had attacked the border post.

As the stench of scorched flesh filled the room, Mr. Gray made to leave. Almost as an afterthought, he stopped, opened the small ink pad on the desk and stamped his passport before strolling out of the burning building.

12

"Are you *really* a bodyguard?"

Connor nodded as he washed down the bitter aftertaste of his malaria tablets with a swig of bottled water.

Henri's eyes widened in awe and he rocked back in his airline seat. "*C'est trop cool!*"

The small yet luxurious eight-seated Cessna plane banked left as they flew over dense jungle toward Ruvubu National Park. The African sun gleamed golden off the aircraft's wings, and the sky was as blue as pure sapphire. Below, the steamy green tangle of trees pulsated with heat and life. Connor could scarcely believe that twenty-four hours earlier he'd been stationed in cold, gray, snowy Wales. But after an eleven-hour flight from Heathrow via Brussels he'd landed in the surprisingly sedate and swelteringly hot airport of Bujumbura, Burundi's capital city. There, he'd joined the Barbier family for their connecting flight to the safari lodge.

Henri leaned forward. "Do you have a gun?" he whispered,

keeping his voice low so that his parents in the front-row seats wouldn't hear.

Connor laughed out loud, thinking of the trouble he'd have had getting one through airport security at Heathrow, even if he had been allowed to carry a gun. "No," he replied.

Henri frowned in evident disappointment. "So how will you protect us?"

"By staying alert for danger, then avoiding it."

"Mais que ferais-tu si tu ne peux pas l'éviter?" asked Amber, who was reclined in one of the Cessna's cream leather seats.

Connor glanced across the narrow aisle at her. As breathtaking as her looks were, Amber acted more frosty toward him than the warmth of her flame-red hair would suggest. She either had forgotten that he couldn't speak her language or was being deliberately awkward.

Having exhausted the extent of his French in the brief and mumbled intro he'd learned by rote for their first meeting, Connor wished he had Bugsy's translation app at hand, but his smartphone was turned off for the flight. With an apologetic smile, he replied, "I'm . . . sorry. What did you say?"

"I said, but what if you can't avoid the danger?" repeated Amber in English graced with a soft French accent.

"Then we'll A-C-E it out of there."

She raised a slender eyebrow in puzzlement. *"A-C-E?"*

Connor was so familiar with the jargon that Alpha team used on a daily basis that he'd forgotten others didn't know the terms. "It's the course of action I'll take to keep you safe. I'll first *assess* the threat, whatever it may be: a shout, a gunshot, or something that raises my suspicions. Then I'll *counter* the danger—either by shielding you or eliminating the threat itself—before we *escape* the kill zone."

"So, as our bodyguard, if someone tried to shoot my sister"—a playful grin sneaked across Henri's face as he formed a gun with his fingers and took aim at Amber—"would you dive in front of the bullet to save her?"

Connor felt a dull ghostlike throb of pain along the scar on his thigh where he'd been shot protecting the daughter of the president of the USA. "If I have to, yes. But with the right security measures in place, it won't come to that."

Henri looked suitably impressed as he fired off several imaginary shots.

Amber pushed aside her brother's finger gun in annoyance. "Papa says Africa is dangerous and that's why we need a bodyguard. But we're not to tell anyone who you really are. Why is that? Surely it would be better if people *knew* we were being protected."

Connor shook his head. "Guardian works on the principle that the best bodyguard is the one nobody notices."

"So, are you the *best*?" asked Amber.

Her piercing green eyes seemed to challenge him, and Connor, still unsure why she was giving him a hard time, was careful how he answered. "Well, I'll certainly do my best to—"

"This is your captain speaking," a voice crackled on the intercom, interrupting their conversation. "We're now flying over the national park. If you look to your right, you'll see the Ruvubu River, after which this park is named. And to your left, our destination and your residence for the next week, Ruvubu Lodge. We'll be landing in a few minutes. The runway is a little bumpy, so please fasten your seat belts."

As everyone strapped themselves in, Connor peered out of the window. Below, the jungle had thinned out into grassy savannah bounded by hills and craggy peaks. He couldn't see the lodge from his side, but the river was clearly visible, a wide meandering stretch of ruddy waterway that divided the park in two.

"Regardez! Regardez!" Henri cried, pointing excitedly at the ground. *"Des éléphants!"*

Connor followed his line of sight and spotted a parade of elephants, with two babies in tow, ambling toward the river. A herd of impala—too numerous to count—grazed in the golden afternoon sun, and zebra and giraffe dotted the landscape. There was no sign of human habitation as far as the eye could see. No towns. No villages. No roads, aside from a few dirt tracks that threaded through the bush like dried-out veins.

Taking all this in, Connor realized that they truly were landing in the heart of Africa.

13

As Connor disembarked from the plane onto the makeshift runway—no more than a dusty strip of cleared land—he felt as if he'd stepped into a blazing furnace. The sudden temperature rise from the air-conditioned cocoon of the Cessna to the intense heat of Africa was almost overwhelming. The sun was so dazzling in the burnished sky that he was forced to squint, and the earth was such a deep red that it looked sunburned. Breathing in the oven-hot air, Connor was hit by the heavy scent of dried grass and wild animals, a rich, earthy smell that was distinctly African.

Shading his eyes, Connor scanned the surrounding area for potential threats. Any nearby wildlife had been frightened off by the noise of the plane. It was just open savannah with a scattering of large flat-top trees. A mile to the north the land rose into a ridge, upon which sat Ruvubu Lodge, commanding panoramic views of the entire plain.

Two brand-new 4×4 Land Rovers were waiting to escort

the diplomat's family and their luggage up the hillside to the lodge. Climbing aboard the rear vehicle with Amber and Henri, Connor was glad of the breeze as they sped along the dirt track. So too it seemed was Amber, who paused in fanning herself with her sunhat.

"Est-ce qu'il fait toujours aussi chaud?" she asked the driver.

Connor hurriedly switched on his smartphone, launched Bugsy's translation app and secretly fitted his wireless earpiece. French was Burundi's second official language after Kirundi, the country's native tongue. If he was going to effectively protect Amber and Henri, he needed to understand what was being said at all times.

"Excusez-moi, madame?" replied the driver as they bumped and lurched their way up the potholed track.

Amber repeated her question. After a couple of seconds' delay, Connor heard through his earpiece: "Is it always this hot?"

"Only during the daytime," the driver replied with a broad grin.

"Well, that's a relief!" Amber laughed, amused by the man's answer.

A few minutes later, their Land Rover pulled up in front of the lodge's grand timber-framed entrance. Several porters rushed to take their bags as they clambered out.

"Bienvenue, Ambassadeur Barbier. Quel plaisir de vous revoir. Comment s'est passé votre voyage?"

After a pause, Connor heard in his ear: "Welcome, Monsieur Barbier. It is so good to see you again. How was your journey?"

Connor was taken aback at the smartphone's almost instantaneous translation. Although the programmed voice was a little robotic, with a bit of concentration he could follow the conversation virtually in real time. It was as if he held a *Star Trek* universal translator in his hand.

"Very good, thank you," replied Laurent in French, shaking President Bagaza's hand as they entered the welcome shade of the stylish reception area, all dark wood and leather armchairs. On the wall behind the reception desk hung the stuffed head of an immense African buffalo, its curved horns polished to a bright sheen, its glass-bead eyes blindly tracking the arrival of the new guests.

A line of smiling men and women, dressed in colorful robes, stood waiting as a welcoming committee.

"It's a pleasure to return to your beautiful country," continued Laurent. "Please allow me to introduce my wife, Cerise."

"Enchanted," said the president, kissing the back of her hand.

"Likewise," Cerise replied with a graceful nod.

Connor had formally met both parents in the airport and chatted with them before boarding the connecting flight. They had been extremely pleasant as well as understanding of the last-minute change in guardian, much to Connor's relief. Laurent had reiterated that he wasn't expecting any problems; he just wanted to guarantee his family's safety during the formal visit. Cerise had seemed a little perplexed at the need for such unorthodox security measures but was reassured to know that her children would have "level-headed" company while the two of them were engaged in their diplomatic duties.

"And these are my children, Amber and Henri," said Laurent.

The president beamed a sunshine of a smile. "Wonderful. I do hope you'll enjoy your stay, children," he said, his voice deep and smooth as molasses. "Ask for anything you want from the staff. You'll be pleased to know that this safari lodge has its own swimming pool—"

"Will we see lions?" interrupted Henri, barely able to contain his excitement.

"Why, of course! The lion is the symbol of our nation," replied the president proudly. His gaze fell upon Connor. "And who might this fine gentleman be?"

"Connor Reeves," replied the diplomat. "A friend of my daughter."

The president shook Connor's hand. He was a big man with a domed head and trimmed mustache. His smile was infectious and his handshake firm and heartfelt. Connor instantly warmed to him.

"You're most welcome to my country, Connor." The president's eyes flicked between him and Amber before he turned to Laurent and quietly remarked, "*Ah, être jeune et amoureux!*"

Connor noticed Amber's brow wrinkle and Henri giggle. A moment later the translation came through in his earpiece. "Ah, to be young and in love!"

Connor decided to play it cool and not correct him. It was to his advantage that the president had gotten the wrong impression, for it would allow him to remain close to Amber without arousing any suspicion about his true role.

One by one, they were introduced to the welcoming party.

First there was Michel Feruzi, the minister for trade and tourism, whose ample bulk rivaled a hippo. Despite being born and bred in Burundi, the heat appeared to affect him too, for he continually mopped his moist brow with a handkerchief. His wife was also on the large side, but she carried herself with remarkable grace and style, her vibrant purple robes only seeming to enhance her imposing presence.

Next was Uzair Mossi, the finance minister, an older man whose tight-knit hair was peppered with gray but whose eyes still sparkled with youth. His surprisingly young wife, a tall, willowy woman with eyes as black as onyx and long braids down her back, stood in stark contrast to Mrs. Feruzi.

Finally they were introduced to Adrien Rawasa and his wife. The minister for energy and mines was a soft-spoken man with a light handshake and an expensive taste in cologne, a fine French musk perfuming the air around him. His wife, Constance, was more forthcoming, embracing the children and presenting Cerise with a gift of a handwoven basket and a beaded necklace.

"Now, Monsieur Barbier, please allow me to give you and your family a tour of the lodge," said President Bagaza. "I want to show you how magnificent this project is. You're our first guests here!"

14

President Bagaza led the way into a lavishly appointed lounge and bar area. Timber framed and thatch roofed, the expansive room was furnished with plush sofas, leather-backed armchairs and a red velvet chaise longue beside a stone fireplace. Floor-to-ceiling glass doors opened out onto a sundeck. In one corner was a wooden tribal mask and in another a handcrafted ivory chessboard. Stretching the entire length of the rear wall was a polished mahogany bar, behind which stood a smartly attired barman putting the final touches to a round of welcoming drinks. And laid out in the center of the hardwood floor was a zebra-skin rug, which Connor noticed Amber sidestep while everyone else strode across with barely a second thought.

"This is a *five-star* luxury lodge," said President Bagaza with a proud sweep of his arm, gesturing at the furnishings. "But I can't lay claim to its construction. That was overseen by Minister Feruzi here."

The president indicated for the minister for trade and tourism to take over.

The minister coughed into his fleshy fist before beginning his spiel. "The lodge features eight glass-fronted, air-conditioned suites, each with a private pool and spectacular views over the Ruvubu Valley. In addition to this lounge, there's a library, a gymnasium and a smoking room, for those less inclined to exercise."

He patted his ample stomach, and a ripple of laughter spread among the gathered party. A second later, once the translation app had caught up, Connor joined in. As the minister continued with his speech, two waiters handed out glasses of iced mint lemonade.

"Along with this cocktail bar, the lodge is blessed with a fully stocked wine cellar, and the dining room offers the finest in French cooking from a world-class chef. Trust me on this—I've sampled it myself."

There was another ripple of polite laughter.

"And, rest assured, the service for guests will be uninterrupted throughout your stay. The lodge has its own electricity generator, and I can guarantee no problems with your phones since a cell tower has been installed. The lodge even has wireless Internet access!"

"We might just move in here permanently," commented Minister Mossi in a half whisper to his young wife.

"Guests will be spoiled by the highest standards of

comfort," Minister Feruzi went on, "and combined with superb game-viewing opportunities, overseen by only the most experienced rangers, this resort promises to deliver the safari experience of a lifetime."

Minister Feruzi gave an affected bow to indicate his speech was over and was rewarded with gracious applause.

"I must say it's very impressive," remarked Laurent, eyeing the sumptuous luxury surrounding them. "Has *all* of France's aid gone into developing this lodge?"

The minister gave a hearty laugh, his jowls wobbling slightly. "No, I can assure you it hasn't. We—"

"Wow, are these *real*?" exclaimed Henri, drifting away from the main group, obviously bored by the adults' conversation. He was pointing to a wall display of a leopard-skin shield and two crossed spears with broad-bladed iron tips.

"Not only real," answered Minister Mossi, joining him by the display, "but once used by the local chief of a Hutu tribe to kill a lion."

Henri stared in wonder at the fearsome weapons.

"Do you want to hold one?" asked the minister.

The diplomat's son nodded eagerly.

"Do you kill everything here?" asked Amber, looking up in dismay at the stuffed head of an antelope on the opposite wall.

Her father shot her a warning look. But Minister Mossi just smiled as Henri brandished the spear. "This is Africa. In

the past, killing a lion was a symbol of manhood. But now"—
he shrugged, taking the spear back from Henri—"attitudes
have changed."

"They most certainly have, Amber. And for the better," assured President Bagaza. "This project is all about conservation. The park has been revitalized, thanks to France's aid.
We've reintroduced lion, elephant, rhino and many other
species—all of which you'll spot on the game drives we have
planned for you. But why not see for yourself now?"

The president ushered Amber and the rest of the party
through a set of glass doors onto the open-air veranda.
There they were greeted by a spectacular view across the
Ruvubu Valley. The African bush was spread out like a gilded
blanket in the midafternoon sun. A natural watering hole
nestled at the base of the slope in which a hippo wallowed.
At the water's edge, several long-horned oryx drank their fill
beside a group of fawn-colored gazelles. A kingfisher flitted
among them, catching insects and dragonflies. Approaching
the watering hole from the south was an elephant and her
calf, and beyond was an abundance of zebra, wildebeest and
buffalo. The scene was like a privileged peek into the Gar-
den of Eden.

Amber was left speechless.

"This is no longer a 'park on paper,' Monsieur Barbier,"
declared the president. "The land has been returned to the
wild. No human habitation at all."

"And with your country's continued support, we intend to establish this as a prime tourist destination," asserted Minister Feruzi, "as well as deliver the discussed conservation and development objectives, of course."

"This is truly magnificent," agreed the diplomat, shaking hands with the president and all the ministers. "The French government will be most pleased with the progress that's been made. Burundi will certainly take its place on the map for this."

The breathtaking beauty of the location had made Connor almost forget why he was there in the first place. Rather than admiring the view, he should have been assessing it from a security perspective. In such a remote and unfamiliar location he needed to be vigilant for all danger, whether from man or beast.

"Can't the animals just wander in?" Connor inquired, unable to spot any obvious protective measures in place.

Minister Feruzi shook his bowling ball of a head. In fluent English he replied, "The lodge is surrounded by an unobtrusive electric fence. It does not spoil the view, but it is effective enough to keep any dangerous animals at bay." He switched back to French. "So you won't be needing that spear, Henri," he said with a wink at the boy.

Trying to make out the fence line, Connor spied movement in a clump of bushes. A soldier in combat fatigues appeared, an assault rifle over his shoulder.

"Who's that over there?" asked Connor, his alert level shooting up as he instinctively moved closer to Amber and Henri.

"One of the presidential guard," replied Minister Mossi. "No need to be alarmed. They'll be patrolling the area around the lodge day and night. You'll barely notice them."

President Bagaza offered his guests a reassuring smile. "I'm so used to their presence that I no longer even see them! Now, please take your time to unpack and freshen up. This evening we're celebrating your esteemed arrival with a boma dinner."

15

Connor laid out the contents of his go-bag on the king-sized bed of his suite. In the rush to prepare for his mission, he hadn't had the chance to double-check his gear. On the flight over, he'd read in the *SAS Survival Handbook* that one's kit could make the difference between success and failure—even life and death.

Usually Amir would set him up with all the necessary equipment he might need for a particular operation. But Connor hadn't even had the opportunity to contact his friend, let alone inform him that he would no longer be providing support. He just hoped that Amir had overcome his initial bout of nerves. Charley was acting as base contact for both of them now. Nevertheless, Connor couldn't help feeling like he was letting his friend down by not being there for him.

It had fallen to Bugsy to supply Connor with his gear, and by the looks of it, his surveillance instructor had done a thorough job. He was equipped with a comprehensive first-aid kit, including emergency antibiotics, syringes and sterile needles—vital in a country with very few medical facilities. There were spare malaria tablets, sunblock and strong insect repellent. He had his sunglasses from his previous assignment—essential for daytime, but equally useful at night because of the layer of nanophotonic film that converted infrared light to visible, enabling him to see in the dark. He also had a rugged flashlight with spare batteries, a portable solar charger for his smartphone and a pair of high-powered compact binoculars. Among his clothes, Bugsy had supplied a stab-proof short-sleeved shirt, cargo pants and a baseball hat with integrated neck shade. But the standard-issue bulletproof jacket would simply be too hot to wear in this climate. He'd have to rely on the go-bag's internal body-armor panel for protection against any gun attack.

The most intriguing item in the kit was a slim blue tube with a drinking spout at one end. A LifeStraw, Bugsy had called it. The device instantly turned muddy puddles into clean drinking water simply by sucking through the tube. With a distinct lack of sanitation in Burundi, the last thing Connor needed as a bodyguard was to come down with a stomach bug or parasitic disease. Small enough to fit in his pocket, the LifeStraw, Bugsy had assured him, removed 99.9 percent of waterborne bacteria and could filter over

275 gallons, enough for one person to survive an entire year.

"Unusual kit for a vacation," said a gravelly accented voice in English.

Connor spun around and saw a stocky man in a khaki shirt and knee-length shorts standing at his open doorway. He wore desert boots and a wide-brimmed safari hat. His suntanned face was rugged, furnished with a goatee, and deeply lined from a life spent outdoors.

"I'm Joseph Gunner," said the man, entering the room and extending his hand in greeting. "But you can just call me Gunner. I'm your park ranger."

"Hi, I'm Connor."

"You're British!" he remarked, somewhat surprised and, judging by the extra squeeze in his handshake, pleased at the discovery.

Connor nodded. "Where are you from? You don't sound or look like you're from Burundi."

"South Africa, born and bred," he replied with a hint of pride. "Used to work in Kruger National Park until I was offered this opportunity." He cast his eye over the gear spread across the bed. "You're more prepared than most tourists. What are you, a Boy Scout?"

"Sort of," admitted Connor, beginning to repack.

The ranger pointed to the knife. "Do you mind?"

Connor shook his head. "Go ahead. It was my father's."

Gunner picked up the knife and examined it. "Well, he's a man who knows his knives. Solid wood handle. Full tang." Eyeing the blade, he carefully ran a finger along its edge before grunting in satisfaction. "There's a saying in bushcraft: *you're only as sharp as your knife.* Glad to see you've kept this one well honed."

Resheathing the blade, he handed it back to Connor, who felt oddly gratified that his father's heirloom was held in such high regard.

"Always important to carry a good knife in the bush," Gunner explained, tapping an impressively large hunter's knife on his hip. The ranger picked up the SAS handbook lying on the bed and leafed through the pages. "You interested in survival skills, then?"

Connor nodded. "More than you might believe."

Gunner smiled. "Well, you've certainly come to the right place to test them out."

16

No Mercy stood guard on an outcrop of rock overlooking the hidden valley. Below, men worked like ants, digging at the earth with shovels and their bare hands. Like layers of peeling skin, the green vegetation was stripped back to expose rocks and mud and, it was hoped, diamonds. Other workers, forced into labor, panned the sediment of the dammed river for the precious stones. They toiled in grim silence, their clothes mud stained and drenched in sweat.

Keeping a watchful eye over their labors, General Pascal's army of child soldiers stood with their guns lazily trained on the men, who were all old enough to be their fathers. Not that any of them thought they needed fathers now that they were warriors of the ANL. No Mercy dimly recalled he'd once had a father, but the general had shown him the weakness of such men. His father had failed to protect his family—had been slaughtered at the hands of a rival rebel group. And now that they were all gone, No Mercy only had himself to fend for, and he wouldn't be as feeble as his father. The general had taught him the power of the gun. And led him onto the righteous path of glory.

No Mercy heard a whoop and saw one man stand up, his arm raised high.

General Pascal, reclining in a plastic deck chair beneath the shade of a palm tree and sipping from a water bottle, beckoned the worker over. The man handed the general his find. Closing one eye, General Pascal held the rock up to the sparkling sunlight and inspected the stone. Even from where No Mercy stood, he could see the reflected gleam and the grin spread across the general's pockmarked face.

Another diamond had been found.

General Pascal waved the worker away, no longer interested, and the man trudged to the makeshift workers' camp, little more than some pieces of canvas strung between the trees. For his valuable find, he'd be rewarded with an hour's extra rest and a double ration of food.

No Mercy, impelled by the call of nature, left his lookout point and found a clump of bushes. Resting his AK-47 against a tree, he found a suitable spot to relieve himself. As he pulled up his pants, he heard a rustle in the bushes. No Mercy stayed very quiet. This was leopard country, after all.

He listened to the noise drawing ever closer. Then he spied movement, and the olive-green uniform of a park ranger materialized out of the bush. The ranger, shouldering a backpack and carrying a rifle, approached the outcrop. The sight of the open-pit mine in the valley below stopped him in his tracks.

Cautiously the ranger backed away from the edge. From his hip he pulled out a two-way radio. Only as he went to switch it on did he spot No Mercy crouching in the bush. For a moment, they stared at each other, neither knowing who was hunter and who was prey.

The ranger offered a tentative smile and put a finger to his lips. No Mercy nodded in obedience.

Reassured, the ranger whispered into the radio's mic, "Echo One to Echo Two, over."

The radio crackled. No Mercy stood, revealing his combat fatigues and the AK-47 in his grip. The ranger's expression went from shock to horror as No Mercy pressed the trigger. Bullets ripped into the ranger's body and he fell to the ground, dead.

The radio, still clasped in the ranger's hand, burst into life. "Echo Two to Echo One. I hear gunfire. Are you okay? Over."

No Mercy stood beside the twitching body of the ranger, watching the blood flow over the edge of the outcrop. He felt no emotion at having killed the man. No guilt. No thrill. Nothing. Just an enveloping numbness. Above the dull ringing in his ears, caused by the thunderous roar of the AK-47, he heard something crashing through the undergrowth.

He spun to see another ranger appear. Without a second's thought, he shot this man too.

The ranger collapsed in a heap. But he wasn't dead—not yet. He made wet choking sounds as he gasped for breath. No Mercy approached, gun in hand, barrel still emitting a wisp of smoke.

"P-please . . . have m-mercy," begged the ranger, holding up a trembling hand in surrender, his eyes full of fear.

"That's not how I got my name," No Mercy replied, planting the barrel on the man's forehead.

"Hold your fire!" ordered General Pascal, appearing with a unit of soldiers.

The boy backed down, not caring whether the man lived or died. He'd done his duty and kept the valley guarded.

General Pascal knelt beside the dying man. "I'm sorry, my friend. My soldier is trigger-happy. There has been a grave misunderstanding."

The ranger nodded, his fingers slick with blood where they clasped at his chest wound.

The general unclipped the man's radio from his hip. "Tell me, where are the other rangers so I can contact them for medical help?"

The ranger shook his head feebly. "No more in this . . . sector," he wheezed.

"No! Then what are you doing here?"

"Looking for . . . poachers."

"There are no poachers here," assured General Pascal, and then his expression hardened. "What are you *really* looking for?"

The ranger's glassy eyes squinted in puzzlement before widening in sheer agony as the general drove the radio's antenna into the open wound. He let out a tortured scream.

"Who sent you?" demanded the general, twisting the radio.

"The president . . ." gasped the ranger, "at the safari lodge."

"Really?" said the general, brightening at the news. Discarding the blood-smeared radio, he rose to his feet and clamped a hand on No Mercy's shoulder. "Excellent work, my young warrior." He took off his red beret and fitted it on the boy's head. "Consider yourself promoted to captain."

No Mercy felt a burst of pride.

"Now take this ranger to the river."

No Mercy's brow furrowed in confusion. "You want me to let him go?"

"In a manner of speaking. Yes. The crocodiles are hungry!"

17

"See anything?" asked Henri eagerly.

Connor lowered his binoculars. After prepping his go-bag for the safari drive the next day and sending a message to Charley to confirm their safe arrival, he'd set off on a security sweep of the lodge. He needed to know the building's layout and where his Principals and the other guests resided. He also had to familiarize himself with the surrounding grounds. Pinpoint where the entrance and exit points were. Locate the park's access roads. Establish routes out in case they needed to make a quick escape. Identify any areas vulnerable to attack or infiltration. And determine what security measures, if any, were in place.

Henri had joined him on this task, thinking Connor was looking for lions and other big game. Amber had still been unpacking and said she'd join them later at the swimming pool. Connor had agreed, as long as she didn't wander off the main site.

"Not yet," replied Connor, passing Henri the binoculars to have a look for himself.

So far what Connor had seen hadn't given him any reassurance. The lodge was the perfect setting for a vacation but a nightmare in terms of close protection. Although their location on the ridge offered unbroken views of the valley and its wildlife, it also meant they were open and exposed. A potential enemy could approach from any direction. And the advantage gained from being able to spot someone a mile off was lost because of the cover provided by the long grasses and clumps of bush carpeting the landscape.

The lodge itself possessed no perimeter alarm system. Nor did it have surveillance cameras. The bedrooms weren't even equipped with fire alarms. And the luxury of the glass-fronted suites was a major liability when it came to providing a safe barrier for his Principals in their rooms—a single gunshot would shatter the entire wall. Connor had inspected the door locks on his own suite and discovered they were flimsy. One hard kick and an intruder could break in with little problem.

The only fixed security measure Connor could identify was the electric fence—a substandard three-wire barrier that encircled the lodge—or at least partly did. He'd already spotted two sections that had fallen flat, stretching the wires to their breaking point. He would have to inform Gunner of this and hope they were fixed quickly.

There were park rangers around, monitoring for intrusion by wild animals. But his key concern was the presidential guard. This should have been their primary ring of defense. Yet the unit of soldiers patrolling the grounds appeared relaxed to the point of negligence. Some were chatting and smoking in small groups, others strolled wearily from one patch of shade to the next, and at least two guards were fast asleep at their posts. Maybe it was the heat, or the lack of obvious threat in such a remote location, but the presidential guard didn't appear to be guarding anything or anyone.

"They're barely in Code White," Connor muttered to himself.

"Code what?" asked Henri, still scanning the bush for game.

"Code White. It refers to a person's level of awareness." He indicated a soldier near the electric fence, picking his teeth with a twig. "See him? He's totally switched off. If someone attacked now, he'd go into shock before being able to react."

Lowering the binoculars, Henri stared at Connor with a mixture of alarm and delight. "Are we going to be attacked?"

"No, very unlikely," replied Connor. "But as a bodyguard, you can't allow yourself to walk around like a zombie. You have to be alert at all times—Code Yellow, we call it. When a possible threat is spotted, you enter Code Orange—a focused state of mind for making crucial decisions, such as wait, run or fight. And if the threat becomes real, then you hit Code Red—basically 'action stations.' But the main thing is you're in control at all times."

Nodding earnestly, Henri began to scan the horizon with renewed intent. "So if I see something I should tell you."

"Yes, but I think you can relax," said Connor, taking back his binoculars. "The likelihood of an armed assault is low. The main threats are going to be from an accidental injury or wild animals."

"Like those monkeys?" suggested Henri, pointing behind Connor to a cluster of giant boulders that marked the top of the ridge.

Turning, Connor saw a troop of large dog-faced monkeys atop a huge rock. "I think they're baboons," he said before spotting Amber clinging to a boulder a few feet below the animals. "What the heck's your sister up to?"

The outcrop of rocks was clearly beyond the safety of the electric fence's perimeter, and he immediately set off toward her. Protecting two Principals at once was always going to be a challenge. But his task wouldn't be made any easier if one of them was a wayward thrill seeker. Crawling under the wire, Connor hurried over, Henri following behind.

"I told you to stay on site. What are you doing beyond the fence?" Connor demanded as Amber effortlessly traversed the rock face. Her hair, red as the African soil, swung free in a long ponytail as she leaned back to assess her route.

"Bouldering," she replied, nimbly switching from one handhold to another.

"Next time, can you tell me if you're going to wander off?"

"Why?"

"It could be dangerous." Connor glanced up at the baboons. They were now making cough-like barks while the younger ones scampered from rock to rock excitedly.

"They're only baboons," she said, hanging from a pocket in the rock by the tips of her fingers.

For such a slender girl, Connor was stunned at her strength. He didn't reckon even the super-tough Ling could manage such a feat.

"You look like a monkey!" cried Henri, jumping up and down, scratching his armpits and whooping.

"And you're just as annoying as one," she muttered. "Can't you go lion hunting or something?"

As Amber worked her way across to the next boulder, one of the male baboons grunted and bared his large yellow teeth.

"I don't think that one's too happy about where you're climbing," Connor remarked.

"Why should I worry?" replied Amber. "I've got you to look out for me."

"That's what I'm *trying* to do."

"Connor's right. You need to be careful, Amber." Gunner

had suddenly appeared behind them. Despite his anti-surveillance training, Connor hadn't even heard the ranger's footsteps. This was the second time Gunner had crept up without Connor being aware of his presence.

"Baboons can be highly aggressive if their territory is threatened," explained the ranger.

Glancing over her shoulder, Amber smiled an apology. "I just needed some exercise after the long flight."

"Understandable . . . but I wouldn't go for that handhold, if I were you," advised Gunner.

Amber frowned. "Why not? Are you a climber?"

"No," said Gunner, picking up a long stick and prodding the crack next to Amber's right hand.

A brown scorpion scuttled out. Amber yelped and dropped to the ground.

"Tempting as it is to go exploring, always bear in mind this is Africa," said Gunner, leading them away from the baboons. "Wild country with wild animals. Just a few steps from the cozy confines of your suite, there's a whole host of hidden dangers."

He lifted up a nearby rock with his boot. A snake slithered out, hissing loudly. Connor yelled out loud in shock and leaped aside as the snake disappeared into the long grass.

Amber barely suppressed a smirk. "Hey, you're white as a sheet. And I thought you were supposed to be a tough guy!"

"I don't like snakes, that's all," Connor replied, his mouth dry with fear. He'd had a phobia ever since an adder had crawled into his sleeping bag on a camping trip with his father and bitten him. He still had nightmares about it.

"Don't fret, Connor. It's just a hissing sand snake. Not poisonous," Gunner explained.

Connor nervously eyed the grass around his feet. "Looked pretty deadly to me."

Gunner shook his head. "Nah, the ones you really have to watch out for are black mambas. Easy to identify by their coffin-shaped head and black mouth. Not only the fastest snake in the world but also one of the most aggressive and poisonous. A black mamba is capable of killing an adult human in as little as twenty minutes. That's why its bite has been called the kiss of death."

"Boys have said that about my sister too!" snickered Henri.

Amber scowled at him.

"Joking aside, little man, the black mamba is the most dangerous snake in Africa," Gunner cautioned. "Believe me, you do *not* want to meet one of those in the bush."

18

Enclosed within a ring of dry reed walls, the boma possessed a magical, almost timeless air. Bleached skulls of antelope and wildebeest marked the entrance. The hard-packed red earth appeared flattened by the tread of generation upon generation of Burundians. And at the heart of the enclosure was a blazing bonfire that crackled and spat orange sparks like fireflies into the glittering starlit night.

Spellbound by the scene, Amber, Henri and Connor sat at one of the simple wooden tables that had been arranged in a semicircle around the ceremonial fire. The other dozen or so guests took their seats in readiness for the evening's entertainment. The only sound in the night, aside from the pop and crack of burning logs, was the ceaseless drone of cicadas. As the insects sang on, waiters appeared with a variety of local delicacies, from red-bean stew to sweet potatoes to *ugali*, a traditional dish made out of corn. These proved to be merely side dishes to a feast of impala, kudu and other exotic bush meats. President Bagaza invited everyone to begin, and as the drinks flowed among the adults, so did the conversation.

"Are you following any of this?" asked Amber in English.

"Some of it," Connor replied. He pointed to his smartphone on the table. "Translation app."

"And I thought you were being spared the pain!" She laughed and peered at the device, impressed. Leaning closer to him, she lowered her voice. "I can't wait to go on safari tomorrow and get away from the adults and all this dull diplomatic talk. But let's see if we can—how do you say in English?—set the cat among the pigeons!"

Connor wondered what havoc she intended. And before he could stop her, Amber had turned to the minister for trade and tourism, who was discussing the expansion plans for the park with her father. With an impish curl to her lips, she interrupted in French, "Tell me, what happened to the people who lived in the park before?"

Her father stiffened at the brazen question. Minister Feruzi smiled graciously, although his eyes turned flinty in the flickering firelight. "They've been given lovely new homes on the park's border, with a school and freshwater wells. Much aid has been invested in the local communities, who will of course benefit directly from the tourism this lodge will attract . . ."

"*. . . this is typical food, Cerise . . .*"

"*. . . besides pottery, basket-weaving is a very popular craft among Burundian artisans . . .*"

Connor tapped at his earpiece. The translation app seemed to be struggling with the multiple conversations happening around the boma. The microphone kept homing in on different people. He fiddled with the settings on the app, switching the mic's sensitivity from "omnidirectional" to "shotgun," enabling him to isolate a single conversation. As he adjusted his smartphone's position on the table to listen to Amber's increasingly heated debate with Minister Feruzi, Connor caught a line of untranslated language through his earpiece. His phone flashed a message, and the app automatically switched from French to Kirundi.

". . . do you believe Black Mamba's back?"

Connor glanced up and saw Minister Rawasa whispering to the gray-haired Minister Mossi on the opposite side of the boma.

"Of course not," snorted Minister Mossi. "I have it on good authority he died in the Congo."

"But what if he didn't? He's the devil incarnate. More poisonous to our countrymen than a real black mamba! His return could trigger another civil war—"

"I tell you, he is dead."

"I've heard it said, no one can kill the Black Mamba—"

Out of the darkness a thunderous beat of drums burst forth, drowning out any further conversation. A line of men clad in white, red and green robes marched into the boma, balancing large drums on their heads. Chanting, they set their instruments down in a semicircle around one central player. Then, to the heavy tribal rhythm, the lead drummer came forward and leaped impossibly high into the air. Whooping and waving his sticks, the man danced as if possessed.

The earth-shuddering beat of multiple drums thrummed in Connor's gut. He'd never experienced such a wall of sound. Another drummer entered the arena and took over the dance. He backflipped into the air, landing with perfect precision and timing. The performance was utterly awe-inspiring as each drummer took his turn in the center. Then, lifting their drums back onto their heads, the procession disappeared into the night, the pounding of drums fading like a receding thunderstorm.

President Bagaza stood and clapped for the performers, everyone else following his lead. When the applause had faded, he said, "Those were the Royal Drummers of Burundi. What distinguishes their music from other African music is that the movement of the dancers dictates the rhythm of the drummers, rather than the other way around. This is another example, Monsieur Barbier, of what makes Burundi unique among African nations. And we *will* beat to a different drum." He raised his glass in a toast: "May Burundi prosper!"

"May Burundi prosper!" repeated everyone, raising their glasses.

With the performance over, the conversations returned to the previous topics.

"So can we go and see this new village you built?" Amber asked Minister Feruzi.

The minister frowned as if irritated, then smiled. "Of course," he replied, "but it'll have to be on another visit."

"Why?"

"I think you've interrogated the minister enough, Amber," her father interrupted, laying a pacifying hand over hers as he noticed Minister Feruzi's frown return.

Amber pulled her hand away. "But I want to meet the people that this park displaced."

"Amber, I realize you're idealistic," said her father under his breath. "But you can't conserve nature without a certain amount of sacrifice."

"But—"

"Enough," warned her father. "I think it's time you went back to your room."

Amber's jaw tightened but she held her tongue. Rising from her seat, she strode out of the boma.

"Can I stay a bit longer?" asked Henri.

"Of course," replied his mother with a smile as Connor got to his feet.

"I'll just make sure Amber gets back to her room safely," he explained.

Leaving Henri with his parents, Connor stepped from the flickering orange glow of the boma into the almost pitch-black of the night. Only a trail of candles lit the path back to the lodge.

Halfway along, he caught up with Amber. She stopped and stared at him. "Why are you following me?"

"I'm escorting you back to your room," replied Connor.

Amber fixed him with a look that said otherwise. "I realize you're here to protect us, but I can look after myself, thank you. And *I'm* not scared of snakes."

Connor felt that remark sting. "Listen, I've trained for over a year in unarmed combat, defensive driving, anti-surveillance, body cover drills—"

"Body cover?"

"Yes, using my body to shield you in an attack."

"Is that your intention with me?" she said, crossing her arms and tilting her head slightly.

"Yes . . . No!" protested Connor, flushing slightly as he realized her double meaning. "Look, I'm just trying to do my job."

"So, tell me, how many people have you protected before us?"

Connor replied, "This is my third assignment."

Amber pouted in disappointment. "Not many, then."

"Well, they're all still alive!" retorted Connor. He took a breath to calm himself. "Listen, I think we got off on the wrong foot. I'm not here to stop you from having fun. I'm here to keep you safe."

"From what?" Amber asked, indicating the tranquil night. "Mosquitoes? It's a mystery to me why my father even employed you. I simply don't need a boy looking after me. If you want to be useful, protect my brother and keep him away from me. Now, good night."

Left openmouthed and speechless, Connor watched her stride off into the darkness.

19

"Those drummers were awesome!" exclaimed Henri, beating at the night air with his fists as Connor led him up the path, the boy's parents having joined President Bagaza and his ministers on the lodge's main veranda.

"I mean, how high could they leap!" Henri jumped into the darkness.

Connor grabbed him before he stumbled into a thornbush. "Careful, Henri—remember what Gunner said. Stick to the path. There might be snakes."

"O . . . *kay,*" he wheezed.

"Are you all right?" Connor asked, hearing the slight whistle to the boy's breath.

"*Fine,*" replied Henri, pulling an inhaler from his pocket and taking a puff. After ten seconds he breathed out, his lungs already sounding clearer. "Just a bit of asthma."

Connor slowed his pace up the hill. From where he was,

he could see the light on in Amber's suite. She'd drawn the curtains, and her shadow flittered across them.

Connor turned to Henri. "Is your sister always so . . ." He tried to think of the most diplomatic word. "Headstrong?"

Henri nodded, sighing in recognition. "And grouchy. Even more so since her boyfriend dumped her last week, for her best friend . . . by text message!"

"That sounds harsh," Connor remarked.

Henri shrugged. "Yeah, well, Maurice was an idiot. I think she's most upset about her friend betraying her, though. She cried a lot about that."

"That's understandable," said Connor. He walked Henri to his room. "See you at dawn for the safari."

Yawning, Henri nodded. "I hope we spot lions tomorrow," he murmured before disappearing inside.

Heading back to his own room, Connor opened the glass door to the private deck and sat in a reclining lounge chair. He gazed up at the blanket of stars overhead. Never had he seen so many in his life. The night was so clear that they truly sparkled like diamonds in the sky.

He glanced over at Amber's suite. The lights were still on, but there was no movement. At least her recent heartbreak explained her frostiness, thought Connor. She'd probably had enough of boys for the time being. And if she knew of her father's past affair, she likely had a trust issue too—especially following the betrayal of her best friend. Connor decided to cut Amber a bit of slack. He'd give her some space. As long as he knew where she was and she didn't wander beyond the lodge's grounds, he could legitimately protect her.

Pulling out his phone, Connor called Guardian HQ to check in for the night. Charley answered within two rings.

After going through formal call-in protocol, she asked, "How are the Cubs settling in?"

Before any mission, specific call signs and code words were selected, since it was always assumed that radio communications could be easily intercepted and no network was 100 percent secure. Amber and Henri had been assigned the call signs Cub One and Cub Two.

"As well as can be expected," Connor replied. "The youngest has accepted its new brother; the older one is a little more resistant."

"What about the Nest?" inquired Charley.

Connor delivered his assessment of the lodge's lax security situation, being careful not to reveal anything too specific that might identify the location.

"Not ideal," she agreed. "But there aren't any storms on the horizon, so you should be okay. Do you have anything else to report?"

"I've heard talk about the Black Mamba coming back. Any idea who this might be?"

"Not off the top of my head, sorry. I'll look into it and get back to you."

"Thanks," said Connor. "It might be nothing, but a couple of the ministers here seemed concerned. How's the bird-watching going, by the way?" he asked, subtly referring to Amir and Operation Hawk-Eye.

Charley lowered her voice as if she didn't want anyone else at HQ to hear. "It's having its ups and downs, but don't worry—our friend hasn't had his wings clipped yet. Tell me, how's your luxury suite?"

"Pretty shabby," Connor replied, reclining farther back in his padded chair. "There are only two showers, and the private pool isn't that big."

"Sounds *horrible*."

"Yeah, but I'll survive."

"We're counting on it," said Charley warmly. "Listen, I have to go. Stay safe."

She signed off. Connor sighed contentedly and returned to gazing at the stars. He always felt better after talking with Charley. More grounded. Talking through the mission helped him put it in perspective. Although the security arrangements were less than perfect, the remote location reduced the risk of direct threats. He thought that he might even be able to relax enough to enjoy the safari tomorrow morning. Connor pocketed the phone and closed his eyes . . . A second later they flew open as a piercing scream shattered the peace of the night.

20

Connor catapulted himself off the chair and leaped from the decking. Pushing through the privacy barrier of bushes, he scrambled onto the neighboring deck. The scream had come from within Amber's suite. It sounded as if she was being attacked, but the curtains obscured whatever was going on inside.

He yanked at the glass door. Locked. He heard another desperate cry. Connor sprinted around to the front. The main door was also bolted. Taking a step back, he front-kicked it with all his might. The lock gave way, and he burst into the room. Amber wasn't anywhere to be seen. Connor's first thought was that she'd been kidnapped. Then another scream erupted from the bathroom.

Throwing open the door, Connor found Amber standing in the middle of the tiled floor, wrapped in a bathrobe, shaking her head furiously.

"Get it off me! Get it off me!"

"What?" said Connor, looking around the room for the threat.

"The spider!"

Connor felt a surge of relief. He'd thought it was something deadly serious.

"Hold still," he instructed, grabbing her by the shoulders and searching her damp locks of hair for the intruder. When he saw it, he jerked away. No wonder Amber was screaming—the spider's body was the size of a golf ball. Dark brown with spindly, hairy legs and two prominent fangs, it was fearsome enough to give anyone a heart attack.

Connor grabbed Amber's hairbrush from the shelf and batted the spider off before it could sink its fangs into her. The creature scuttled across the tiles at a horrific speed. Amber yelped again and leaped into the bathtub for safety.

Gunner ran in. "What's going on?" demanded the ranger, looking between Connor and Amber, still dripping wet from her shower.

"Spider," explained Connor, pointing to the creature now scurrying up the wall.

Gunner eyed it, whipped off his hat and plonked it over the offending arachnid.

"Just a rain spider. Nothing to worry about," he said, picking up a magazine and trapping it inside his hat. "Relatively harmless. They hunt at night and sleep during the day. They can bite, but their venom's no more dangerous than a bee sting . . ." He glanced at Amber, trembling in the bathtub. "Granted, though, they look bloody terrifying."

Amber nodded mutely, her eyes not leaving Gunner's hat for a second.

"It's the small black-button spiders with red underbellies you need to avoid like the plague," warned the ranger, checking the bathroom for any other creepy-crawlies. "They have one of the most toxic venoms produced in nature, fifteen times stronger than a rattlesnake's. You'll probably know them as black widow spiders—" He was interrupted by two soldiers from the presidential guard appearing at the door.

Better late than never, thought Connor.

"False alarm," said Gunner to the soldiers, and they wandered back outside, muttering to themselves.

Gunner held up his hat cheerily. "Well, Amber, that's your official welcome to Africa. All clear now."

He headed for the main door and spotted the damaged lock. "I'll have someone fix that tomorrow. Oh, and remember to shake out your boots before putting them on in the morning. You don't want any other nasty shocks."

He disappeared into the night to release the eight-legged intruder.

Connor turned to Amber. "Will you be all right?"

Quickly recovering her composure now that the spider was gone, she pulled her bathrobe closer around her and shooed him out of the bathroom. "Yes, absolutely."

There was a flush to her cheeks, and she wouldn't quite meet his eye. But as she closed the door on him, she smiled shyly. "At least you're tough enough to fight off spiders."

21

Dawn had barely broken, and the sun, low on the horizon, cast a golden sheen across the wakening savannah. A few zebra glanced up from their early-morning grazing as the convoy of Land Rovers bumped their way along the dirt track, sending up clouds of dust into the warm, still air.

In the lead vehicle Connor sat next to Henri, who was fidgeting with excitement, his head darting left and right like a meerkat's as he searched for animals. Stifling a yawn from the impossibly early start, Amber steadied herself in the front seat beside Gunner, who was at the wheel. Although there was ample space, Laurent and Cerise had elected to go in the second vehicle to give their children the freedom to enjoy the safari alone. The other four Land Rovers transported the president, his ministers, their wives and a detachment of the presidential guard.

Perched on the hood of Connor's vehicle in a lookout seat was their tracker, Buju, a quiet man with soulful eyes and a shy smile. Upon introduction, Gunner had spoken for him, explaining that Buju had grown up in the Ruvubu Valley, lived off the land by hunting and gathering, and that he knew every gully, waterway and crevice of the national park like the back of his hand. Buju would be their eyes and ears on the safari.

From the man's watchful gaze and calm, almost still, presence, Buju appeared very attuned to his environment, and Connor realized it would be hard for any predator to sneak up on them without their tracker noticing. Despite this assurance, Connor didn't allow himself to lower his own guard. Although it was good to have another pair of eyes on the lookout for danger, his Principals' safety ultimately lay with him.

Buju held up his hand and the safari convoy came to a halt. Gunner killed the engine. Behind, the other five drivers did the same, and the rumbling of motors ceased, to be replaced by a chorus of birdsong, buzzing insects and the occasional braying of zebra. The sound track of Africa. Then in the distance they heard a haunting *whoop-whoop*.

"Hyenas," Gunner explained under his breath. "A long way off, probably in those hills." He indicated a far ridge, crowned by the rising sun.

"So why have we stopped?" asked Henri.

Gunner put a finger to his lips to silence him as Buju pointed to a clump of thornbushes about fifty feet ahead.

Amber craned her neck to see what the tracker had spotted, her camera at the ready.

"What is it?" whispered Henri, rising to kneel in his seat.

Amber shook her head and shrugged. Then out from behind the thicket emerged a creature as gray as slate, with an immense barrel body and stumpy legs, its sloping neck and low-slung head finishing in a large, pointed double horn. Like a creature straight out of *Jurassic Park*, the rhino appeared truly prehistoric. It tramped into the middle of the dirt track and stopped, suddenly sensing them.

Connor, Amber and Henri stared in awestruck silence.

Gunner kept his voice to barely above a whisper. "You're very fortunate to see a black rhino in the wild. Their species have been driven to the point of extinction. Less than five thousand are left in the whole of Africa."

The rhino stood stock-still, only its ears twitching, and then it swung its head toward them, snorting at the air.

"Rhinos have poor eyesight but an excellent sense of smell and hearing," continued Gunner as Amber began shooting away with her camera. He pointed to a small red-billed bird on the animal's back. "That's an oxpecker. It was thought that they removed ticks and insects for the benefit of the rhino, as well as providing an early warning system by hissing and screaming if a predator approached. But more recent research suggests these are actually bloodthirsty bodyguards."

Amber looked back at Connor and raised an eyebrow.

"Rather than eat the ticks, the oxpeckers have been seen removing scabs and opening fresh wounds to feed on the rhino's blood," explained Gunner. "So, although it's in part a mutually beneficial relationship, the oxpecker is also a parasite."

Connor hoped Amber didn't consider him a parasite. He'd been careful to keep his distance and focus on Henri when they'd been prepping for the dawn safari. And since the spider episode the previous night, he'd noticed she had become more open toward him.

They watched as the little bird pecked with its red beak at the rhino's rump. The rhino twitched and turned slowly, until its back was to them. Then it excreted several huge dollops of dung that plopped onto the ground in a steaming heap.

"Gross!" exclaimed Henri.

"Well, that's certainly put me off my breakfast," agreed Connor.

Gunner grinned. "An adult rhino can produce as much as fifty pounds of dung in a day. Did you know each rhino's stool smell is unique and identifies its owner? They often use communal dung deposits, known as middens, to serve as local message boards. Each individual dung tells other rhinos who's passed through, how old they are and whether a female is in heat. Think of it like a post on one of your social networks."

"That's a pleasant image!" said Amber, laughing.

Having done its business, the rhino trotted off and disappeared into the thicket.

"What a spectacular start to the safari!" declared Gunner, switching on the Land Rover's engine. "Your first close encounter with one of the Big Five, and it's only six a.m."

"What are the other four?" asked Amber.

"Elephant, lion, buffalo and leopard. Can't guarantee we'll spot a leopard, though. They're pretty elusive."

Henri frowned. "Why isn't a hippo one of the Big Five? Surely it's larger than a leopard."

Gunner shook his head. "It isn't about size. The 'Big Five' was the term used by colonial hunters for the five species considered the most dangerous to hunt. Although you're technically right, a hippo should be on that list. Hippos kill more people than any other animal in Africa."

"Really? What about mosquitoes?" said Amber.

"Yeah, I'll give you that. They're responsible for millions of deaths through the spread of malaria. But mosquitoes aren't directly attacking you, unlike hippos, who are fiercely territorial. I can assure you, you *don't* want to get between a hippo and water. But if you really want to be picky, then there's one beast in Africa that's killed more than all the mosquitoes, hippos, elephants, crocs and lions combined."

"Which one?" asked Connor, intrigued.

"The most deadly species on Earth," said Gunner, fixing him with a grave look. "Man."

22

A single fan whirred like an oversized mosquito in the corner of the makeshift office, no more than a lopsided whitewashed brick hut with a corrugated tin roof, on the edge of a Rwandan border town. The fan's feeble breeze was barely enough to stir the stifling air as the diamond merchant, a thin-faced man with half-moon spectacles and a shirt two sizes too big, removed the stone from its bag. He deposited it under the microscope with the infinite care of a parent holding a baby for the first time. Then, setting aside his glasses, he peered through the eyepiece.

"A pink, very rare . . . and desirable," he said, adjusting the focus and magnification. "Clarity is almost flawless, at least internally."

The merchant pulled back and blinked, as if he couldn't believe the quality. Retrieving his spectacles, he glanced up at the client sitting opposite him. The white man hadn't moved a muscle since taking his seat. Yet his posture suggested he was ready to strike like a panther at the slightest provocation.

"Where did you get this?" asked the merchant breathlessly.

"I'm not paying you to question," said Mr. Gray. "I'm paying you to appraise."

"Of course," replied the merchant, immediately returning to his work. No stranger to violence, the merchant recognized the implied threat in the man's tone and had no intention of antagonizing him further. With due diligence, he transferred the stone from the microscope to a set of digital scales. The merchant tried not to show any surprise at the reading, but it was impossible to hide the shocked dilation of his pupils.

"A little over thirty carats, in its rough state," announced the merchant, somehow managing to keep his voice even.

"Estimated value?"

The merchant licked his lips as he considered the rare diamond before him. "Twenty million dollars, if not more."

Mr. Gray nodded, picked up the stone and laid out ten hundred-dollar bills on the table. "For your appraisal. Plus another ten for keeping your tongue." He added more bills to the pile. "Or else I'll return to *take* your tongue."

"Discretion is my religion," assured the diamond merchant, pocketing the money. As his client reached the doorway, he cleared his throat. "You'll have trouble getting that stone out of Africa without the correct certificates. I could h—"

"That's my concern, not yours," said Mr. Gray, stepping out into the hot midday sun.

He crossed the potholed road to his battered Land Rover. Once aboard, he pulled a phone from his pocket and dialed. A voice answered, slightly distorted by the encrypted line. "Status?"

"The stone is legit. Twenty million, minimum."

"A satisfactory investment, then," said the voice. But Mr. Gray couldn't tell whether the person on the end of the line was pleased or disappointed by the figure. "Have you secured means of export?"

"Yes, I'm meeting the contact in six days for transport to Switzerland, where it will be KP-certified."

"Fine work, Mr. Gray. Everything else on schedule?"

"Ahead, by all accounts. The coup appears imminent. The general's hungry for war. He's contacted me for more weapons."

"That's easily enough arranged. But can we trust him to stand by our agreement?"

"He knows the score if he doesn't," Mr. Gray said. "But the general is a loose cannon—no ethics and no boundaries."

"Sounds like the ideal candidate to ignite chaos," replied the voice. "What's the status of the opposition?"

"Unprepared, according to my source. But its army is well enough equipped. I would anticipate heavy losses on both sides."

When the voice replied, the pleasure was unmistakable this time. "A fight between grasshoppers is always a joy to the crow."

23

"*Safari* is Swahili for *journey*," explained Gunner, grabbing a small backpack from the rear of the Land Rover. "And the only way to truly experience Africa is on foot."

It was now afternoon, and the ranger had offered to take them on a walking safari. Enticed by the prospect of such a unique opportunity, Laurent and Cerise had decided to join them, the president and his entourage having returned to the lodge.

Connor shouldered his go-bag, which contained his water bottle, insect repellent, the first-aid kit and other critical supplies. In the side pockets of his cargo pants, he stowed his smartphone and LifeStraw and, on his hip, his father's knife. Although they were being guided by an experienced ranger and tracker, Connor was taking no chances. In the SAS survival manual, he'd read *always to expect the unexpected*—a motto equally relevant to a bodyguard's philosophy. And, without the backup of the presidential guard, he wanted to be prepared for any eventuality.

Henri was protesting loudly as his mother smothered him in SPF fifty sunscreen. Amber, in shorts and a T-shirt, her hair tied back by a bandana, rolled her eyes at her younger brother's complaining. After applying some lip balm, she picked up her camera and water bottle, eager to get moving. Connor was just putting on his sunglasses and baseball hat when the diplomat approached.

"How's the trip so far?" he asked.

"All going very smoothly," replied Connor. "Nothing out of the ordinary to report."

"It seems my fears may have been unfounded," admitted Laurent, admiring the glorious expanse of open savannah. "Still, it's good for Amber to have someone around her own age. She's been a little down recently. Perhaps you can cheer her up? Keep her occupied while I'm involved in diplomatic discussions."

He gave Connor a pointed look, and Connor recalled the awkward conversation between Amber and Minister Feruzi at the boma dinner.

"I'll do my best," said Connor, sensing the diplomat wasn't aware of his daughter's recent breakup.

Once everyone was ready, Gunner drew the group together. "A few basic rules for this safari. Follow my instructions at all times, without delay or debate. Stick together and walk in single file. No talking, unless we're gathered to discuss something of interest. And if we do happen to confront any dangerous game, whatever you do, *don't* run. You'll trigger the hunting instinct and become prey. Remember, you're not in a zoo. This is Africa."

"Are you sure we'll be safe?" asked Cerise, putting a protective arm around her son.

"Haven't lost anyone yet," replied Gunner. "Though you are our first guests!"

He smiled to show this was a joke, then thumbed in the direction of a young park ranger, who wore a rifle slung over his shoulder. "Don't worry, Mrs. Barbier, Alfred's here to protect us."

Gunner nodded at Buju to lead the way, and Laurent, Cerise, Amber and Henri followed in single file, with Connor and Alfred taking up the rear. They tramped through the long grass in silence. Although Connor's baseball hat shielded him from the blazing sun, the ground itself radiated heat like a mirror, and within minutes of the trek, he was drenched in sweat.

All around, the savannah buzzed with life. Insects flitted from bush to bush, guinea fowl squawked as they scurried for cover, and brightly colored birds darted between the trees dotting the landscape. The air, no longer tainted by the Land Rover's exhaust fumes, was heavy with the scent of animal dung, dried grasses and the dust kicked up from the baked red earth.

The whole experience was totally different from riding within the safe confines of the Land Rover. Connor felt exposed and, for the first time, vulnerable. He was suddenly aware that they were on an equal footing with all the other animals in the park. Were it not for Alfred's rifle, they'd be poorly equipped to defend themselves against lions and other predators with teeth and claws.

At the same time, he felt a thrill at being so immersed in the wild. His senses seemed sharpened, and he was alert to even the tiniest of details: a column of black ants marching across their path, the scrunch of dried grass beneath their boots, and a shiny beetle rolling a ball of dung three times its size up a slope. This was Africa in its rawest form.

Buju came to a halt beside a clump of thornbushes. Gunner beckoned the group to join them. Peering over, they spotted a bull elephant feeding on the leaves of an acacia tree. Henri's eyes widened at the sheer size of the animal no more than thirty feet away from them.

"The largest land-living mammal in the world," explained Gunner under his breath as the elephant entwined its trunk around a branch and ripped off the leaves, the twigs crackling in its grip. "They can spend up to sixteen hours a day foraging for food. The trunk is remarkable. Made up of over a hundred thousand muscles and no bones, it can tell the size, shape and temperature of any object. And its sense of smell is four times more sensitive than that of a bloodhound. Thankfully, because of Buju's guiding skill, we're downwind of this one."

"It's magnificent," Cerise remarked as Amber focused her camera and took a photo.

"What would happen if he noticed us?" asked Connor, the thornbush seeming an ineffective barrier against an elephant charge.

"Most elephants are understandably wary of humans and will move off," Gunner replied. "But if threatened it would stomp the ground, fan out its ears and raise its head. However, you know you're in real trouble when it pins back its ears, curls its trunk and issues a loud trumpeting. That means it's about to charge. And for their bulk, elephants are extremely fast and surprisingly agile. If on foot, as we are, I'd advise making for the nearest tree or embankment. Elephants seldom negotiate those obstacles."

"Are the elephants protected within this park?" asked Amber, taking another photo.

"They're as safe as in any other national park," said Gunner. "They have no natural predators, apart from man, of course. But they've developed an extraordinary ability to differentiate between humans. They can tell a man from a woman, an adult from a child—all from the sound of a human voice."

"What about poaching?" asked Laurent.

"Armed rangers patrol the different sectors. However, with ivory fetching up to thirty thousand dollars per pound—more than gold and platinum—I admit poaching is still a massive problem." Gunner sighed heavily. "The poachers of today are well resourced and heavily armed. A few will be rich Europeans and Americans seeking the thrill of the hunt, but most are locals looking to make a quick buck. Organized crime gangs, rebel militia and even terrorist organizations are getting involved. But we're fighting back, thanks to the funding from countries like yours." He nodded toward the elephant. "And if this one, with tusks his size, can survive this long, we're doing a good job."

Having had its fill of the acacia tree, the elephant lumbered off. Buju waited until the animal was a good distance away before continuing the safari. In single file, they crossed a dry riverbed and passed a herd of impala. The wind shifted slightly, and the herd started as they caught the human scent. Buju paused beside an enormous tree that looked as if it had been planted upside down. The trunk was over twenty feet in diameter and towered some sixty feet above them, where the leafless branches spread out like a profusion of roots in the sky. From these hung velvety pods the size of coconuts.

"This is a baobab tree," said Gunner, patting the massive trunk. "Otherwise known as the tree of life."

"Why's that?" asked Cerise.

"For both wildlife and the local population, the baobab is a vital source of shelter, clothing, water and food. The bark is fire resistant and can be used for making cloth and rope. The fruit"—he pointed to the hanging pods—"can be broken open and eaten raw. Its flesh, somewhat crumbly and dry, is packed with vitamin C. The seeds can be ground into coffee. And, if you're thirsty, just cut out little sections of the trunk's inner bark and suck them to get the moisture out. Mature trees are also often hollow, providing ideal shelter, and traditionally the children of Hadza tribe are born inside a baobab tree. So, with very good reason, it's called the tree of life."

As they rounded the colossal trunk, they were met by a cloud of black flies. They buzzed around the remains of a carcass that lay festering in the sun. The stench of rotting meat was overpowering and made Connor and the others gag.

"What's that?" asked Laurent, holding his hand over his nose.

Gunner knelt down and inspected the ravaged remains. "A gazelle."

"Poor thing," remarked Amber.

"In Africa only the strong survive," Gunner said. "Every morning, a gazelle like this wakes up and knows it must run faster than the quickest lion or it will be killed. And every morning a lion wakes up knowing it must outrun the slowest gazelle or it will starve to death. So, it doesn't matter whether you're a lion or a gazelle in this life; when the sun comes up, you'd better be running."

24

"Did a lion kill this gazelle?" asked Henri, fascinated by the fly-infested carcass.

"Most likely," replied Gunner. Then Buju said something and pointed to a patch of sandy ground. "Hang on, I might be wrong."

They gathered around the tracker, who was crouched on his haunches.

"See track here?" said Buju softly. "Four toes, no claw marks, rear pad with three lobes. That's the spoor of a big cat."

Henri glanced up at Connor, his eyes wild with excitement.

"It's relatively small and circular in shape, so indicates leopard," said Buju.

"A *leopard* killed the gazelle?" gasped Henri. "I'd love to see a leopard!"

Buju pointed to another set of prints. "Here are lion tracks."

"How can you tell?" asked Connor, unable to spot any difference.

"More oval and larger, because of the animal's weight."

The tracker's eyes scanned the ground as if reading the scene that had played out. He waved a hand east. "Leopard made the kill on the plains. Dragged the gazelle here." He indicated the wide scuff marks and broken grass. "Tried to carry his kill up the tree, but three . . . no, four lions chase leopard off." He drew everyone's attention to the cluster of paw marks by the base of the trunk. "Then hyena come and drive away lions."

"They look the same as leopard tracks to me," remarked Laurent.

"No—see the claw marks," said Buju, his finger tracing the tiny points by the toes. "And only two lobes on the pad. Definitely hyena."

"So which way did the leopard go?" asked Henri eagerly.

Buju cast his eyes around, then pointed northeast to a craggy peak in the distance, atop which stood a single acacia tree. "That way, toward Dead Man's Hill."

"Sounds like a pleasant place for a picnic," remarked Amber as she took a close-up of a lion print.

"It's a known haunt for the leopard," Gunner explained. "Locals have always been fearful of the hill and its adjoining gorge. Superstition says those who venture there never return. But let's see if Buju can track these prints for a little while. We might get lucky enough to come across the leopard if it's settled in a tree, or otherwise the lions who stole its kill."

At Gunner's suggestion they swapped places in line to give everyone a chance up front, and Connor found himself behind the ranger. They trekked in silence as Buju paused every so often to examine the ground before heading off again, sometimes in a different direction.

"Buju can read the bush better than anyone I know," Gunner whispered over his shoulder to Connor as the tracker studied a clump of grass. "By following tiny traces, he gains a sense of the animal's direction, then assesses the landscape as a whole to gauge where it may have gone next, before searching for another sign. It's much quicker than following each track one by one."

"What sort of things is he looking for?" asked Connor.

"Grass that's been trampled down. Vegetation that's been broken or bruised. Soil or rocks that have been disturbed. But where he really comes into his own is aging the tracks. Buju can determine how long it's been since the animal passed by simply from how dried out a broken leaf or stem is, or by the moisture in the ground beneath a disturbed rock. A good tracker is like an expert crime-scene investigator."

After half an hour of tracking with no sighting of a leopard or a lion, Henri declared, "I'm hungry."

"But we only recently had lunch!" his mother said, and sighed.

"Not to worry," said Gunner, bringing the party to a halt. "Out in the bush there's always food. You just need to know where to look."

He led them over to a fallen acacia tree, put his ear to the trunk, listened, then pulled back the bark. The rotting wood was infested with white wormlike creatures.

"Rhino-beetle larvae," said Gunner in delight, picking out a plump one between his fingers. "Cooked, they're a bush delicacy, but you can eat them raw."

"You've got to be joking," said Amber, eyeing the creature with disgust.

Gunner shook his head. "Pound for pound such insects contain more protein than beef or fish; they're the perfect survival food."

He held the bulbous wriggling larva in front of Henri's nose. The boy grimaced. "I think I'll pass."

"Fair enough. But I'm sure you eat honey, and that's been regurgitated by bees countless times. So this food's no more unsavory." Gunner popped the larva into his mouth and began chewing. "I have to admit, though, rhino-beetle larvae do taste a bit like boogers!"

Henri snickered as the ranger washed down his live snack with a swig from his water bottle.

"If that doesn't appeal to you, then you could try termites," Gunner suggested, heading over to a tall earthen mound. He plucked a long grass stem and fed it into one of the small holes in the structure. "These are an excellent food source, and if you chuck a piece of termite nest onto the embers of a fire, it'll produce a fragrant smoke that keeps the mosquitoes away."

He tugged the stem from the hole, which was now swarming with pale brown ant-like insects.

"Connor, perhaps you'd like a taste?" said Gunner, offering him the stem.

"I'm not *that* hungry," Connor replied, waving a hand at the persistent flies that buzzed around their heads.

"You can't be too choosy in the bush."

"Go on," urged Amber, her green eyes watching his reaction.

Not wishing to be thought of as a wimp, Connor took the stem and ate a mouthful of termites. He felt the little insects crawling all over his tongue. After a couple of quick chews, he swallowed, swearing he could feel them wriggle down his throat. "They taste like . . . dirt," he admitted.

"But they're fresh!" said Gunner with a grin. "Fried, the termites have a lovely nutty flavor. Well, if that's not to your liking, we could always hunt for snake."

"*Snake?*" exclaimed Connor, his stomach turning at the thought.

"Yeah, a snake is steak in the bush!" Gunner laughed. "Sixty percent protein, and that means energy."

"But aren't most of them poisonous?" questioned Laurent.

"Only the end with fangs. Chop off the head, sling the body on some hot coals, skin and all, and you've got yourself a hearty meal. The only problem is killing the snake in the first place without getting bitten!"

He turned back to Henri. "So what will it be—larva, termite or snake?"

His face a little pale, Henri replied sheepishly, "Um . . . I was hoping for something along the lines of a chocolate bar . . ."

25

"They're not doing very much," whispered Henri as he crouched with the others, peering through Connor's binoculars. The pride of four lions lay listless under the shade of a tree, their tails flicking every so often at the buzz of flies.

Amber looked sideways at her brother and tutted. "You're never satisfied, are you? Buju's guided you to lions and all you can do is moan."

"But on TV they're hunting or doing something exciting," Henri muttered. "Not just *sleeping*."

"Well, why don't you go for a run and see if they'll chase you?" suggested Amber with a sardonic smile.

"I wouldn't if I were you," cut in Gunner. "Lions are mostly nocturnal hunters, resting up to twenty hours a day, but they'll still attack if they spot an opportunity. And you'd make a fine snack, Henri."

"If lions hunt for themselves, why did they steal the leopard's kill?" questioned Laurent.

"Because out of every five attempts a lion will only make one kill. That's why scavenging is a vital food source for them."

"I feel sorry for the leopard," said Cerise. "It did all the work and these lions reaped the benefit."

"Don't be. Leopards are the great survivors," said Gunner. "They may be slower than a cheetah and weaker than a lion, but they'll beat them all in the end." He pointed to the grassland surrounding them. "At this very moment there could be a leopard only a few feet away from us and we wouldn't even know."

As if there'd been a sudden drop in temperature, the atmosphere within the group became tense as their eyes darted from bush to grass to shrub, wondering if there *really* was a leopard nearby.

"They're superbly camouflaged hunters. They're also excellent swimmers and climbers, and they can leap long distances," Gunner went on. "A male leopard can drag a carcass three times its own weight—including small giraffes—up a tree. No prey is safe from a leopard. Believe me, of all the cats, a leopard is the most cunning and dangerous. The perfect predator."

"Would they ever attack humans?" asked Cerise anxiously.

"Absolutely," replied Gunner. "A leopard is easily capable of killing any one of us. It might drop out of a tree or pounce from behind a bush, then seize you by the throat and suffocate you between its jaws." Connor could see that the ranger was enjoying the looks of horror on their faces. "Leopards eat whatever form of animal protein is available, from termites to snakes to waterbuck. But when there's a shortage of regular prey, a leopard may resort to hunting humans. A few are *true* man-eaters, having gotten their taste from scavenging on human corpses during the civil war. Such leopards are truly to be feared."

Connor and the others were stunned into silence. The savannah no longer seemed a perfect paradise—rather it felt like a hunting ground where *they* were the prey.

Gunner checked his watch. "Well, time to head back," he announced cheerily. "Dusk is only an hour off. And we don't want to become dinner for these lions."

With uneasy looks at the surrounding trees and bushes, Connor and the others hastily followed him. Buju led the way, guiding them back along the banks of the Ruvubu River. The late-afternoon sun had turned the waters golden, and hippos wallowed in the meandering current, snorting and making strange *muh-muh-muh* sounds. Every so often Connor would spot the snout and black slit-eyes of a crocodile as it broke the water's surface. A few basked on mud banks, their saw-toothed jaws wide open.

"Those crocs are trying to cool off as they sweat through their mouths," explained Gunner. "They have the strongest bite of any animal in the world and one of the quickest too—

able to snap their jaws shut around prey within fifty milliseconds!"

"It seems everything in this country is lethal," remarked Connor.

Gunner laughed. "Survival of the fittest, my friend. Oddly enough, though, the muscles that open a croc's jaws aren't so powerful. A reasonably strong person like yourself could hold a croc's mouth closed with just his bare hands. The problem is that most victims never see the croc coming, since it uses surprise rather than speed in an attack. That's why you should never take water from the same spot twice on a river. Crocs watch you the first time, then get you the next—"

"Ow!" cried Amber.

Connor spun, fearing the worst. Then he saw that her camera strap had become entangled in a thornbush. Amber struggled to free herself but merely became more entwined within its branches.

"Careful, that stuff's like barbed wire," said Gunner, heading back along the trail to help her. "It'll rip your clothes to shreds, as well as your skin."

With great care, the ranger began to work her free, unhooking the thorns one at a time. Connor tried to help too, but only succeeded in pricking his own thumb.

Amber gritted her teeth as the thorns scratched at her bare skin.

"Sorry," said Gunner. "This is why it's called a wait-a-while bush. The South African Special Forces used it to snare prisoners and keep them from escaping."

"I can believe that!" said Amber, inspecting the blood seeping from her cuts.

When she was finally free, Connor took out an antiseptic wipe from the first-aid kit and offered to clean up her scratches. She willingly let him hold her arm and wipe off the blood. Amber smiled at him—her first with genuine warmth. "Thanks."

"Anytime," replied Connor, putting his first-aid kit back in his go-bag.

"Right, let's move on," said Gunner.

"Wait, where's Henri?" asked Cerise.

Connor glanced around. The boy was nowhere to be seen. Connor had been so absorbed in tending to Amber's cuts that he hadn't kept an eye on her brother. He cursed his lapse of concentration.

"*Henri!*" called his father. But he got no answer.

Connor retraced their steps down the trail. But the tall grass and thick undergrowth meant anyone straying even a few feet from the path could easily disappear from view and become lost.

"Buju and Alfred, spread out," instructed Gunner. "Everyone else stay with me. We don't want to lose anyone else."

Cerise started to sob. "You don't think he's been taken by a"—she glanced at the bushes—"a leopard?"

"Don't fret, Mrs. Barbier," said Gunner. "He probably just wandered off. My men will find him."

But it was Connor who spotted Henri first, through a gap in the bushes. He was standing on a mud bank overlooking the river. A crocodile's head broke the surface.

"Henri! Stay back from the water!" shouted Connor, rushing over to him, the others close behind.

"I found another dead gazelle," said Henri, oblivious to the panic he'd caused and the predator eyeing him.

Connor peered over the lip of the bank. A carcass was washed up at the water's edge. It wasn't much more than a bloodied rib cage with a few flaps of skin hanging off. Then Connor realized the skin was actually khaki colored and made of cloth.

"I don't think that's a gazelle," said Connor, drawing Henri away from the dismembered corpse.

26

"A dead body isn't exactly good PR for the park," said Minister Mossi sarcastically, turning his gaze on Minister Feruzi, slouched in the leather armchair of the lodge's smoking room. "Come to Ruvubu, swim with man-eating crocodiles!"

"It wasn't a crocodile that killed the man," said Gunner, who stood beside the stone fireplace, his safari hat in his hands.

"What do you mean?" said President Bagaza, stiffening in his chair.

"He was shot first. *Before* the crocodiles ate him."

Minister Feruzi stubbed out his cigarette in a silver ashtray. "How did you come to that conclusion?"

"Buju found a bullet embedded in the rib cage."

A haze of tobacco smoke hung in the air as the president and his ministers sat silent, contemplating this fact.

"So do we know who the victim is yet?" asked Minister Rawasa quietly. "A local villager?"

"Impossible to tell for certain, considering what's left," replied Gunner, his expression grim. "But I am guessing it's either Julien or Gervais. The khaki cloth matches our park uniform, and both rangers have failed to report back."

"This is a disaster! The last thing we need on Monsieur Barbier's first visit." The president got to his feet and gazed pensively out the window across the valley. "Who do you think did it?"

"Poachers, most probably."

"What sector were the two rangers patrolling?" asked Minister Feruzi, lighting up another cigarette.

"Sector eight, northeast," replied Gunner.

"Keep your men clear, Gunner."

Gunner frowned. "What about catching these murderers?"

"We will. But wait until we have the necessary reinforcements."

"It'll likely only be a small group of poachers," pressed Gunner. "I can lead a unit of rangers; while their tracks are still fresh, Buju can follow them to their camp."

"Let *us* decide on the best course of action," said Minister Feruzi firmly.

Gunner's jaw tightened. The president came over and laid a reassuring hand on the ranger's shoulder. "I promise you,

Gunner, we will find these criminals. But your job is to ensure the French diplomat and his family have the best safari possible." He led Gunner toward the door. "When you do confirm the body's identity, pass on my condolences to any relatives, and if the victim has a wife, inform her that she'll be suitably recompensed for her loss."

"Yes, Mr. President."

"Oh, and, Gunner," called Minister Feruzi, "I'd advise against saying anything to the diplomat and his family at the moment. Leave that to us. No need to worry them unnecessarily."

"Understood," said Gunner before leaving the room.

When the door closed, President Bagaza looked to his ministers. "So, how should we handle this?"

Minister Feruzi coughed into his fist. "Tragic as it is, a dead ranger might give us leverage in requesting more aid to combat poachers."

"I don't think that's the point here," responded the president. "What if the rangers stumbled across the diamond field and paid for it with their lives?"

"We should send in a unit of soldiers to search sector eight," suggested Minister Mossi.

"Isn't that a bit of overkill?" argued Minister Feruzi, flicking ash from his cigarette.

"I agree," said Minister Rawasa. "We don't want the diplomat spooked by an increased military presence."

"I hear you all," said the president, "but the priority is to secure any diamond field within the park. If the rumored return of Black Mamba is to be believed"—he glanced around at his ministers—"we need to take steps *now* to protect our country's interests."

27

"They're insisting there's nothing to worry about," Connor relayed to Charley back at HQ. "A tragic accident, but one they say is all too familiar over here."

"I suppose swimming in a river has its dangers, especially within a national park full of wild animals," replied Charley, her image pixelating on the phone's screen as the Internet connection slowed. "Do they know who the victim is?"

Connor shook his head. "They're guessing it's a local."

"You don't look so convinced."

Charley read him too well. "I get the sense they're hiding something. Or at least not telling the whole truth," he explained, keeping his voice low even though he was alone in the lodge's reception area. He walked over to the entrance just to make sure. "I didn't study the corpse for too long, but bits of clothing looked very much like the park rangers' uniform. Plus our ranger appeared more concerned than I'd expect him to be for someone he didn't even know."

Charley pursed her lips thoughtfully. "Maybe there is more to it, but remember this safari is meant to be a good-will exercise for the Burundian government. They probably want to gloss over the incident and move on. How are the Cubs taking it?"

Connor glanced back into the lodge's lounge area, where Henri was playing a game on his phone and Amber was reading a book. "Only the youngest got a good look. He's a little shocked but otherwise fine. Cub One kept her distance. I think the parents are more upset than they are, the mother in particular. But Cub Two is already asking when the next outing will be."

"And when is it?"

"Tomorrow: a sunset safari. The tourism minister suggested we spend the day enjoying the pool before heading out."

"Well, let's hope this next trip's a little less eventful. By the way, I've pulled some information on the snake you mentioned."

Connor felt his stomach tighten. And by the grave look on Charley's face, he had every reason to be concerned.

"Black Mamba is the nickname for the notorious rebel fighter General Pascal," revealed Charley. "Born in Burundi, he began his fighting days at the age of sixteen, alternating between being a rebel and a soldier both in his own country and the Democratic Republic of Congo. At the age of eighteen he joined the FDD—Forces pour la Défense de la

Démocratie—but deserted them a few years later to wage war on behalf of the Union of Congolese Patriots. Eventually he founded his own rebel group, the ANL—Armée Nationale de la Liberté—who gained infamy almost overnight for killing three hundred refugees in a United Nations camp on the Burundian border. Most of the victims were women, children and babies, beaten with sticks, shot dead or burned alive in their shelters."

Connor sat down heavily in one of the reception's leather armchairs. "He sounds like a monster."

"That's barely scraping the surface," Charley said, sighing. "His group attacked the capital, Bujumbura, leaving three hundred dead and twenty thousand people displaced. He sparked a rebellion that led to several massacres amounting to genocide, and it set back the peace process by several years before the ANL were defeated and pushed back into the Congo. Responsible for countless atrocities, the Black Mamba has also been indicted by the International Criminal Court for recruiting child soldiers."

"Children?" said Connor, almost unable to believe what he was hearing. "Kids like us?"

Charley nodded solemnly. "His tactic was to abduct them and force them to kill their own parents. Those who refused were beaten to death. Those who obeyed had sacrificed all ties to home and family. With nothing to go back to, their new family became the ANL."

"But why children?"

"Because children are easier to condition and brainwash," replied Charley. "Also, child soldiers don't eat as much food as adults, don't need to be paid and have an underdeveloped sense of danger, so they're easier to send into the line of fire."

Connor was struck by some of the parallels to their own situation. But *he* hadn't been forced to become a bodyguard. And he'd been trained to save lives, not kill and murder.

"That's why General Pascal was nicknamed the Black Mamba," continued Charley, "for being the most dangerous and poisonous 'snake' in Africa. He is a ruthless and evil man. Or I should say, *was.* All reports indicate the general died in the Congo two years ago. However, there's no hard proof. That's why I'm recommending to Colonel Black, based on the concerns of the ministers you overheard, that we up the threat status of Operation Lionheart to Category Two."

The significance was not lost on Connor. In operational terms, this meant the threat was considered real and could conceivably happen.

"Keep a close watch over the Cubs, Connor . . . and stay safe. You're in wild country."

Connor slapped at a mosquito on his neck. "Don't I know it," he muttered, pulling his hand away to see a smear of his own blood.

28

The full moon, bright in the coal-black sky, silhouetted the skeletal acacia tree atop Dead Man's Hill and cast a ghostly sheen on the valley below. Like discarded trash, clusters of men and boys were curled up beneath the scant shelter of ripped canvases, each and every one of them too exhausted to care that their beds consisted of little more than rocks and dirt. In the darkness at the edge of the makeshift camp, a handful of rebel soldiers kept watch—not for danger but for any worker attempting to escape.

A little farther upstream, General Pascal paced outside the entrance to his tent, swigging from a bottle, a satellite phone clamped to his ear. Blaze sat nearby, sharpening his machete while listening to rap on a pair of oversized headphones. Beneath the spluttering light of a kerosene lamp, No Mercy played cards with Dredd and two other boy soldiers, Hornet and Scarface, the rickety makeshift table threatening to collapse as the dog-eared cards were slammed down with gambling zeal.

"I win," declared Hornet, reaching forward to claim the cash.

Dredd clamped a hand over the winnings. "No, you cheated!"

"You want to argue with me?" said Hornet, standing up to his full height and flexing his formidable muscles.

With a scowl, Dredd pulled back his hand and began dealing afresh as Hornet sat down and counted his prize money.

"Let them come," said General Pascal into his phone. There was a pause as he listened. "Don't fret. We have the firepower, and more is on the way. Besides, it will all be over by tomorrow."

Ending the call, the general turned to Blaze, who lifted one ear of his headphones away, music blasting out.

"A unit of government soldiers has been sent to search this area," explained the general. "So from dawn I want scouting patrols in all sectors. Understood?"

Blaze nodded and glanced over at No Mercy and the others. "You hear that, boys?"

They all saluted in acknowledgment, then resumed their game. But they'd barely gone a round when a bloodcurdling scream echoed through the valley, followed by shouts of panic.

General Pascal discarded his bottle and grabbed his gun. Abandoning their card game, No Mercy and the others raced after the general and Blaze to the source of the cries. They found the enslaved workers huddled together, their eyes wide and fearful as they stared into the pitch-black interior of the jungle.

"What happened?" demanded General Pascal, sweeping the undergrowth with his Glock pistol.

"The idiots just started screaming," replied one boy soldier with a shrug.

Blaze backhanded the boy. "You were supposed to be keeping watch!"

As the boy nursed his split lip, a rake-thin worker stammered, "It—it . . . took him."

"Who?" demanded General Pascal.

"Jonas," replied the worker.

"No, *not* the man," spat the general in disgust. "The attacker. Did you see who it was?"

The worker shook his head, but another proclaimed, "It was an evil spirit. A skin walker!"

A spasm of fear rippled like a wave through both workers and soldiers alike.

"This valley is cursed!" wailed a voice.

Others started moaning softly to themselves as the panic began to spread.

"It was no evil spirit," corrected an elderly man, his voice low and reverential. "It was a leopard. The largest I've ever seen."

He pointed a gnarled finger to some rocks and then a tree. Shimmering in the moonlight, a trail of slick blood was the only evidence of the prisoner's disappearance.

"A man-eater!" General Pascal breathed in awe.

All eyes went to the jungle, the supernatural fear of spirits hardening into an instinctive terror of the wild. A big cat with a taste for human flesh prowling their valley meant no one was safe.

"This is a bad omen," muttered Dredd.

"No! This is a *good* omen," corrected General Pascal with a smile as white as bleached bone. "The leopard is by far the most cunning of killers."

Crouching down, the general dipped his index finger into the blood of the leopard's victim, then daubed the sign of the cross in red on his forehead.

"Blood has been let. But not from one of our soldiers, for we are the chosen ones," he declared, now painting upon the brows of No Mercy, Dredd, Hornet and his other foot soldiers. "For we are the hunters, not the hunted."

29

"Dusk is one of the best times to spot predators," Gunner explained to Amber, Henri and Connor as they drove with the safari convoy toward a ridge in the distance.

Although sunset was still a couple of hours off, the late-afternoon light was already transforming the savannah into a bronzed mythical landscape. The red-rich earth seemed to glow with warmth, and the Ruvubu River flowed like molten gold through the sweeping expanse of the national park. As the convoy bumped and weaved its way across the rolling landscape, Buju, strapped into his seat on the hood, drew his young passengers' attention to many of the wondrous sights surrounding them: a parade of elephants lumbering toward a watering hole, their enormous ears flapping like great sails; impalas and antelopes leaping into the air as if dancing for joy; towers of giraffes striding regally between clumps of acacia trees; and a mighty herd of black buffalo, their hooves dredging up clouds of red dust as they thundered away from the approaching Land Rovers.

Although the mood at the start of the safari had been a little more subdued than the previous occasions, the discovery of the dead body still on everyone's minds, the Eden-like wonders of the park soon pushed aside any somber thoughts. In awe of the sheer diversity of wildlife, Amber eagerly snapped away with her camera while Henri searched the savannah for lions on the hunt, desperate to see a real kill in action. Even Connor had his smartphone out, filming some of the more impressive animals to show the rest of Alpha team, back in cold snowy Wales, what they were missing.

"Look! A cheetah!" said Gunner, slowing the Land Rover and bringing the convoy to a halt.

Buju was pointing into the near distance where a distinctive black-spotted form was slinking through the long grasses toward a herd of antelope. Totally oblivious to the predator stalking them, the antelopes continued to graze contentedly in the golden sunlight. Suddenly the cheetah burst from its hiding place in an explosion of speed. The antelopes scattered in panic. Weaving and zigzagging, its tail whipping this way and that, the cheetah bore down on its chosen prey—a young buck. The antelope switched direction again and again, trying to shake off its pursuer, but despite its valiant efforts the cheetah was faster and more agile.

It knocked down the buck with a swipe of its claws, then pounced on its throat. The antelope struggled in its viselike grip, but was soon suffocated.

"That was awesome!" Henri exclaimed, grinning from ear to ear.

Amber glanced over her shoulder at her brother in the backseat beside Connor. "Satisfied now?"

Henri nodded excitedly. "That was about the *best* thing I've seen in my whole life. I can't wait for a lion kill."

Amber sighed. "Haven't you seen enough dead bodies for one vacation?"

"Are you kidding?" replied Henri, using Connor's binoculars to watch the cat devour its prey.

She gave him a despairing look before returning to face the front.

"It's just part of the circle of life, Amber," said Gunner. "Life and death go hand in hand in Africa." He paused, staring off into the distance, before continuing: "More often than not, a cheetah will fail in its attack. It may be the fastest land animal in the world, but it tires quickly."

"How fast can a cheetah run?" asked Connor.

"Up to seventy miles an hour in around three seconds. That's quicker than most sports cars."

Connor was astonished. With the "show" over, the convoy set off again.

Keeping one hand on the wheel, Gunner leaned over to Amber. "I think the sunset will be more to your liking. The viewpoint we're going to is a photographer's dream."

Cresting a hill, he indicated the small plateau they were heading for. As the convoy dropped down into a dried-out riverbed as wide as a four-lane highway, its tree-lined banks forming steep slopes on either side, Buju held up his hand for them to stop again. He dismounted from his seat and walked over to a patch of sandy ground. Crouching, he inspected the earth.

"What's Buju spotted now?" whispered Amber.

"I'm not sure," replied Gunner, switching off the engine.

Behind, the other five Land Rovers—transporting Laurent and Cerise, the president and his guard, and the ministers and their wives—switched off their engines too and waited. After a minute or so, Buju beckoned Gunner to join him. Clambering out of the driver's seat, he went over and began studying the ground with the tracker.

The vehicle now stationary, the muggy heat of the late afternoon pressed in on Connor and the others. Batting away the ever-present flies, Connor looked up into the cloudless sky and saw a vulture hovering overhead. For a moment he imagined himself the prey and felt a chill run down his spine.

"What do you think they've found?" asked Amber.

"Lion tracks?" suggested Henri optimistically.

"Maybe leopard," said Connor, scanning the surroundings as Henri's eyes widened at the thought.

The rest of the convoy was strung out along the broad riverbed, the rear vehicle a good distance back, still on the bank. Laurent and Cerise were listening intently to their ranger, who was pointing out a striking red-and-yellow bird in the branch of a tree. The driver in the president's vehicle was craning his neck, wondering what the holdup was, while the Burundian ministers and their wives in the other 4×4s appeared hot and bored.

For some reason Connor's sixth sense began twitching. All around, the land seemed unnaturally still. Maybe the presence of the vulture had spooked him. Or maybe it was because they were in the sweltering hollow of a riverbed. But he couldn't hear any birdsong; even the insects had stopped chirping. Connor knew from what Gunner had told him that when the bush went quiet, it was a sure sign that a predator was about.

He scanned the clumps of tall grasses, dense scrub and nearby trees for movement or anything unusual, but his eyes weren't trained to spot the telltale signs of hidden wildlife, a skill that would be second nature to Buju or Gunner. Then a glint of reflected light at the base of a bush caught his eye. Retrieving his binoculars from Henri, Connor focused the lens on the undergrowth, and his breath stopped dead in his throat. A pair of eyes, cold and calculating, stared right back at him.

Connor saw intelligence in those eyes. And in that instant he knew they were all in grave danger.

30

"What did you see?" asked Henri excitedly.

All of a sudden a lone impala bolted from behind a clump of tall grass. At the same time, a short sharp *crack* punctured the silence. Pivoting in his seat, Connor spotted the president's driver slumped over his wheel. For a moment Connor thought he was just resting, but then he noticed the splatter of fresh blood on the Land Rover's windshield. A second later the president's 4×4 rattled as if being pelted by hail.

"GET DOWN!" yelled Connor, shoving Henri to the floor of their vehicle and throwing his go-bag on top of him, its body-armor panel acting as a shield.

The ferocious roar of heavy gunfire filled the air, and Amber screamed, frozen where she was like a startled deer. Realizing she had "brain fade," Connor threw himself into the driver's seat and forcibly pushed Amber's head down just as their windshield shattered under a strafing of bullets, glass raining down on them.

"What's happening?" cried Amber, her whole body trembling as Connor tried to shield her, a shard of glass having cut her cheek.

"It's an ambush," said Connor.

He risked raising his head for a moment to take stock of the situation. From the banks on either side, the black barrels of a dozen AK-47s protruded from the bushes, their muzzles flaring with gunfire. President Bagaza was cowering in his vehicle, his presidential guard all but decimated. His personal bodyguard lay across him, a bullet through the head, while two other guards hung limp out of the doors, their blood dripping into the sand. The unit of soldiers in the backup vehicle were firing indiscriminately at their hidden adversary, pulling the trigger with panic rather than accuracy. Only their driver seemed to have his wits about him as he restarted his engine, floored the accelerator and raced to rescue the president.

As more bullets peppered their own vehicle, Connor recalled Jody's number one rule in an ambush situation: *always keep moving.*

Buju and Gunner were nowhere to be seen, so it was down to him to get them out of the kill zone. Twisting the keys in the ignition, Connor heard the engine turn over but fail to start. He tried again. It sputtered, then died. Connor cursed but waited a moment, afraid of flooding the engine. Hearing a shrill *whoosh*, he braced himself as a rocket-propelled grenade screeched overhead. A second later, the finance minister's Land Rover exploded in a ball of flames. Their own vehicle rocked with the force of the blast.

"Mama! Papa!" screamed Amber, rising up from the floorboard.

Connor pushed her back down. "It wasn't *their* car," he shouted, trying the ignition once more. The engine whined, then kicked into life. *Third time's the charm,* he thought.

The stench of burning diesel now filled the air, and a column of black smoke billowed into the sky.

"Stay down," Connor instructed Amber and Henri as he sat up and grabbed the steering wheel. He went to put the Land Rover into gear and found the door handle instead. Only then did it dawn on him that the driver's seat was on the left-hand side of the vehicle. In Britain it was the other way around. Battling the mental confusion of using his right hand on the gearshift, he crunched the Land Rover into first gear and floored the accelerator. The tires kicked up dirt, then gained traction and shot forward. Laurent and Cerise's Land Rover was already ahead of them, the driver hunkered down low as he sought to escape the lethal ambush.

Connor followed close behind, forcing the Land Rover into second gear and keeping to the other driver's tire tracks. With the steep banks corralling them in, they had no choice but to head upstream. The worst of the firefight was still concentrated on the president's vehicle and his remaining guard. But just as Connor dared hope they might make their escape, the front tires of the Barbiers' Land Rover were shot out. The driver lost control, hitting the bank, and the vehicle flipped over. It crashed directly into their path. Connor wrenched the steering wheel hard left. They swerved, barely missing the upturned Land Rover and almost overturning themselves. In the back, Henri squealed as he was flung from one side of the floor to the other.

"Do you *know* how to drive?" Amber shouted, clinging on for dear life, unable to see the chaos unfolding.

Connor nodded. "Sure—passed my test last week," he said, shooting her a nervous smile.

But that knowledge didn't seem to reassure her. He was about to slam on the brakes and return for her parents when a gunman in faded army fatigues rushed out from behind a tree, an AK-47 targeted on their vehicle.

Connor realized it would be a death sentence if he stopped. Ducking behind the dashboard, he accelerated hard. The gunman stood his ground, emptying his magazine into the charging Land Rover. Over the roar of the engine, Connor could hear the impact of bullets pinging off the steel bull bar at the front. As the 4×4 picked up speed, the gap between them and the gunman rapidly closed, and for one horrible moment Connor thought the man wasn't going to move. Then, with death almost upon him, he leaped aside.

But too late.

Connor heard a heavy *thunk* as the Land Rover's bull bar caught his trailing leg. In the side mirror, he saw the man writhing on the ground, alive but out of action. He also glimpsed the Barbiers' vehicle, smoke rising from the engine compartment. There was no sign of life from its occupants.

Connor kept his foot flat on the accelerator, telling himself that his priority was Amber and Henri. Not their parents. He hated having to make such a ruthless decision, but he knew that if he turned back now, they'd all be slaughtered.

Rounding a bend and leaving the carnage behind, Connor spotted a route up the bank and headed for it. He was concentrating so hard on driving that he failed to notice the deep trench running from one bank to the other. Only at the last second did he slam on the brakes, and the Land Rover came skidding to a halt just short of the ditch.

His heart thudding in his chest, Connor desperately searched for another way out. But with its steep tree-lined banks, the riverbed made the perfect choke point for an ambush. Once the trap had been sprung, there was no escape.

31

Gunmen rushed out to surround the Land Rover. But Connor refused to surrender without a fight. With the engine revved to the max, he threw the gearshift into reverse and sped away from the trench. It was a desperate decision to head back into the kill zone. But it was his only option.

The gunmen opened fire, and bullets thudded into the retreating Land Rover.

"You're going the wrong way!" yelled Amber, her face pale, blood trickling from the cut to her cheek.

"Just taking a little detour," he explained. "Hold on, you two!"

Taking his foot off the pedal, he spun the steering wheel hard right and yanked on the hand brake. The Land Rover went into a spin. But Connor's planned J-turn quickly turned into a disaster. Driving on dirt rather than concrete, the 4×4's tires weren't as slick, and the vehicle pivoted only halfway before stopping abruptly. The Land Rover keeled over like a ship capsizing in a storm as Connor and his two Principals clung to anything they could grab. For one terrifying moment the vehicle threatened to flip onto its side. Then it lost momentum and righted itself, landing on all four wheels with a bone-jarring crunch.

Shaken but unhurt, Connor released the hand brake and spun the wheel the opposite way. As he fought to turn the Land Rover fully around in the unforgiving dirt, the gunmen bore down on them. More rounds peppered the bodywork, shattering the right side-view mirror and shredding one of the headrests. As they drew closer, Connor got his first good look at their attackers and was shocked to see that some were boys around his age. One boy in a black bandana, hefting an oversized assault rifle, was firing with wild abandon into their vehicle as if he were playing a video game.

The glazed, deadened look in the boy's eyes was even more disturbing, spurring Connor to get out of there. With a crunch of gears, they shot off along the riverbed and back around the bend. As they raced past the Barbiers' upturned Land Rover, Amber poked her head up and desperately searched for her parents. The vehicle was now on fire, tendrils of flame and smoke licking the undercarriage. The roof was half crushed, blocking their view of the rear compartment. When Connor caught a glimpse of a bloodied lifeless arm hanging from the driver's window, he held out little hope for Laurent or Cerise. Their park ranger was sprawled a few feet from the wreckage. Judging by the footprints in the dirt, he'd survived the crash, but not the bullets through his chest.

Connor drove on, and Amber slumped back onto the floor of the vehicle. Ahead he saw that President Bagaza had been evacuated to the backup vehicle, the only functioning Land Rover left, apart from their own. But he and his guards were under heavy fire. And with little cover to protect them, they were being slaughtered. Bodies lay everywhere, the dry riverbed now flowing freely with their blood.

Connor dared not stop. His only goal was reaching the dirt road the convoy had come in on. Passing the blazing, twisted shell of Minister Mossi's Land Rover, he tried not to look at the burning bodies inside. The other Burundian ministers, who'd been at the rear of the convoy, weren't anywhere to be seen, and Connor prayed they'd somehow escaped this bloodbath. All of a sudden the ground in front of their Land Rover erupted as a rocket-propelled grenade shot past and detonated. Rocks and debris rained down, red dust obliterating all visibility. Driving blind, Connor instinctively swerved, narrowly avoiding the smoking crater before bursting out of the cloud of dust. Then they were tearing up the bank and leaving the sound of gunfire behind.

However, just as Connor thought they were in the clear, two flatbed jeeps appeared, blocking their escape.

"Brace yourselves!" Connor shouted to Amber and Henri, both now mute with terror.

Dropping into second gear, Connor accelerated hard up the slope. The gunmen in the jeeps began firing at them. Connor kept going. The Land Rover struck the roadblock, smashing into the front fenders of both vehicles. The men on the backs of the jeeps were flung off. The Land Rover's bull bar crumpled but did its job of saving the engine from being crippled. Connor pushed on through, metal scraping on metal as the two jeeps were shoved aside. With a final roar of the engine, the Land Rover burst free and tore off down the road.

32

"What happened back there? Who was shooting at us? *Why* were they shooting at us?" babbled Amber, propped up in the passenger seat, the wind whistling through the broken windshield and whipping at her red hair.

"I don't know," said Connor, focusing on the dirt road ahead. "All I know is we have to put some distance between us and them. Are you hurt?"

Amber put a hand to her cheek. "I don't think so . . . . It's just a little cut."

"Good. Henri, how about you?"

Her brother didn't answer.

"*Henri?*" Connor repeated louder. "Speak to us." He glanced into the rearview mirror but couldn't see him. He prayed the boy hadn't been shot.

Amber clambered around in her seat and looked down to where her brother lay huddled on the floor in back. "Henri, are you all right?"

She turned to Connor. "He's not responding."

"Can you see any blood?"

Amber shook her head. "No, he looks fine."

"He's probably in shock," explained Connor.

Amber reached toward her brother and gently shook him. "Henri, are you okay?" She shook him again. "He's nodding."

Connor breathed a sigh of relief. It was a miracle all three of them had escaped without injury. Then he noticed a patch of blood staining the left-hand side of his T-shirt. He felt no pain, but the adrenaline was probably masking that.

"Our first priority is getting back to the lodge," he announced, deciding not to examine his wound any further. Whether it was serious or not, they couldn't risk stopping so close to the ambush site. "That'll be the most secure location. At least until Guardian can arrange a flight out of here."

"But we can't just . . . leave," stuttered Amber, her voice cracking with emotion. "M-my parents . . ."

Connor kept his eyes on the road, unable to meet her pleading look. "If they escaped, that's where they'll go too," he replied.

"*If?*"

"Pass me my phone," he instructed, wanting to avoid the topic, at least until they were out of immediate danger. He indicated the backseat, where he'd dropped it in the rush to protect her. Amber numbly reached behind her, and it was this action that saved her life. A bullet ripped through her headrest, missing her neck by a fraction. More lethal rounds zinged past.

"They're following us!" she yelled, sliding down low in her seat.

In the rearview mirror, Connor saw a jeep hurtling along the road, a dust cloud billowing up in its wake. Connor increased speed, urging the Land Rover to go faster. The whole chassis shook as the dirt road punished the 4×4's suspension. He wrestled with the steering wheel, his bones jarring as they hit pothole after pothole.

Another bullet ricocheted off the dashboard, and a glance behind told him what he feared most. The gunmen were gaining on them. And they were still miles from the lodge. Realizing the odds of outrunning their pursuers were close to zero, Connor made the decision to head off-road.

"Where on earth are you going?" said Amber, baffled by his seemingly crazy actions.

"The jungle," he replied, nodding toward the trees bordering the savannah. "We'll try to lose them in there."

Connor weaved between the bushes at high speed, taking advantage of their cover. As they bounced and rocked over the rugged terrain, he almost collided into a boulder, then narrowly avoided a clump of trees. He simply ran straight over any small thornbushes, their branches screeching and scraping at the undercarriage.

"Watch out!" cried Amber.

A herd of impala bolted in fright, leaping across their path. Connor swerved madly to avoid hitting them. Behind the Land Rover, the sound of gunfire drew ever closer, but he didn't dare look back again for fear of crashing. Cresting a slope, the Land Rover cleared the ground and came down with an almighty thump. Part of the exhaust system fell off, and the engine began roaring like a lion. Caught in a deadly game of hide-and-seek with his pursuers, Connor drove on for all he was worth toward the sanctuary of the jungle. The undergrowth thickened around them, and for a moment he believed he'd shaken them off. Then a blast of bullets pulverized a nearby tree trunk, bark and splinters flying into their path.

Connor swung the Land Rover hard right, following what appeared to be animal trails deeper into the jungle. Sunlight flickered through the canopy overhead, and the encroaching undergrowth slapped at the vehicle's sides. They quickly lost sight of their pursuers. Then without warning the ground dropped away and the Land Rover tipped forward. It hurtled out of control down a sheer slope, bouncing off rocks and careering through bushes. Connor, Amber and Henri were flung around the cabin, powerless to stop their breakneck descent. A massive tree loomed up in front of them and the Land Rover came to a violent, shuddering halt, the hood crumpling like cardboard as they struck the trunk head-on.

Groaning in pain, Connor pressed the palm of his hand

to where he'd hit his forehead on the steering wheel. Blood was seeping from a gash above his left eye. He was dazed but alive. Amber was slumped next to him, her head lolling on the door frame.

"Are you okay?" he asked, laying a hand on her shoulder.

Amber let out a soft moan. "I think so," she managed to reply. To add to the cut on her cheek, she now had a split lip, countless grazes and a dark bruise along her thigh.

"Anything broken?"

"Yes . . . my camera." She held up the shattered remains. "But I'll survive."

Clambering out of the vehicle, Connor's legs gave way beneath him and he had to drag himself back to standing. He peered into the rear compartment. Henri was curled up in the fetal position on the floor.

"How about you, Henri?" Connor asked, gradually feeling his strength and senses returning.

Henri gave him a thumbs-up. Connor smiled. From what he could see, Henri's position had protected him from the worst of the crash, although he was going to sport some pretty impressive bruises. Connor held out his hand and pulled Henri from the wreckage, before going to help Amber out through her window.

Surveying the scene, Connor discovered that he'd driven into a hidden ravine. The Land Rover was totaled, the crash having broken the front axle and torn off the left-hand wheel. The only way they'd be getting to the lodge now was on foot.

Reaching inside the vehicle, Connor retrieved his go-bag. He also found his binoculars jammed against the door. But, worryingly, there was no sign of his phone. He had leaned in farther through the window to look under the seats when suddenly the jungle erupted with the sound of gunfire. Connor dived behind the nearest tree, dragging Amber and Henri with him. The gunmen were now at the top of the ravine, shooting blindly into the bushes. With no time to grab anything else, Connor propelled Amber and Henri forward, and the three of them fled for their lives.

33

"It's hard to dodge a spear that comes from behind!" growled President Bagaza.

He knelt in the bloodstained sand, his hands bound but his head held high. The unexpected appearance of Black Mamba, still alive, had shocked him and his surviving guards. But he was determined not to show any weakness in front of his lifelong adversary.

General Pascal sneered and prodded the president's belly with the tip of his boot. "You've gone soft while in office, Bagaza."

"You're still the coward you always were, Pascal. Killing innocent women and children. And when you can't kill them"—the president glanced over at No Mercy—"you use them to fight your own battles."

General Pascal laughed. "As if *you* haven't committed enough of your own crimes! Your hands are as dirty as mine."

"At least I've tried to wash them of my sins. I've brought

this country back from the brink," argued the president fiercely. "Are you determined to plunge us back into civil war *just* to line your own pockets with diamonds?"

"Why not? You appear to have done well enough from the last war. Now it's my turn. I've decided to run for president."

President Bagaza couldn't hide his astonishment. "But . . . no one will vote for you! Not the Black Mamba."

"Are you so certain?" The general turned to his rebel soldiers. "Who thinks I should be president?"

Every one to a man and child raised their hands.

"How about my old friend here?" he said, patting President Bagaza amiably on the shoulder.

All the hands dropped.

General Pascal offered his opponent a conciliatory smile. "Election over. You lose."

He drew his Glock 17 pistol and shot President Bagaza straight through the eye. The president flopped backward into the dirt. Holstering his gun, the general stepped over the lifeless body of his enemy, then strolled up the bank.

"What about the prisoners?" asked Blaze, waving the barrel of his AK-47 at the row of terrified guards.

General Pascal considered them for a moment, then said, "Give them a choice of long or short sleeves."

The guards exchanged horrified looks as Blaze produced his machete. Two gunmen seized the first guard in line, and the rebel fighter indicated the elbow or wrist as to where he'd hack the man's limb off. As the guard began begging for mercy, a jeep skidded to a stop at the top of the riverbank. A soldier jumped out and saluted the general. "We caught up with the first vehicle but lost the children."

"How could you *lose* three children in a Land Rover?" demanded General Pascal, his tone exasperated.

"They drove into a ravine," explained the soldier.

General Pascal gave a snort of amusement. "Are they dead?"

The soldier shook his head. "They disappeared into the jungle."

The smile evaporated from the general's face. "My orders were explicit. No one must be allowed to escape. No one can raise the alarm."

The general turned to Blaze. *"Hunt them down!"*

To be continued . . .

Turn the Page for a Sneak Peek at

Book 6 : Survival

"Are you sure we're going the right way?" asked Amber, panting from the exertion of their trek.

The jungle had thickened, and progress had become painfully slow as they tramped through dense undergrowth and clambered over rotting tree trunks. Mosquitoes buzzed in their ears, a constant irritation despite having doused themselves with insect repellent. In the treetops, monkeys chattered unseen and leaped from branch to branch, sending leaves falling like rain onto the earth below.

Connor wiped the perspiration from his brow and checked his compass again. It was proving impossible to keep to a straight bearing, because trees, ferns and vines choked the jungle floor, forcing them to constantly alter course.

"We need to head to higher ground," he said. "Work out where we are."

Coming across an animal trail, he led them upslope. The

light was fading fast, and the jungle was being swallowed by shadows. Soon they wouldn't be able to see one another, let alone their pursuers. Henri, his eyes darting toward any strange sound or movement, was becoming more and more scared, and he didn't protest when his sister took his hand. The terrain beneath their feet grew rockier as they ascended toward a small ridge, the trees thinning as they climbed. Suddenly, as if they were emerging from a deep dive, the canopy parted to reveal an indigo-blue sky, the first stars of night blinking in the heavens.

Standing atop the rocky ridge, Connor was able to look out across part of the Ruvubu Valley. Using his binoculars, he tried to spot any familiar landmarks. The sun, a ball of fiery orange, was burning low on the horizon, giving him true west. To the south, the Ruvubu River wound lazily through the valley basin. And off to the east, he could make out the craggy peak of Dead Man's Hill. The dried-out riverbed where the ambush had taken place was hidden from view by the trees, but Connor was able to figure out the lodge's rough direction from a single dark line that cut across the savannah. With so few roads, the main dirt track stood out like a scar on the landscape.

"We're a little off course," he admitted, directing their gaze to a midpoint in the distance. "That's where the lodge is. Somewhere on the other side of that ridge."

Amber squinted into the twilight. "How far, do you think?"

"At this pace, half a day's walk, I guess, maybe more."

Amber glanced at her brother, who was wheezing again from the climb. "We need to rest," she said.

Connor looked at both Henri and Amber. They were all tired, hungry, hot and thirsty. They'd been running on adrenaline and shock for the past hour. Now that that was beginning to fade, their bodies were crashing. He nodded in agreement. Finding a patch of clear ground, they sat down and Connor retrieved the water bottle from his go-bag. Barely a couple of gulps remained. He offered the bottle to Amber, who let her brother drink first. Then, after taking a sip herself, she handed it back.

Despite his own thirst, Connor waved the bottle away. "You have it."

"No," insisted Amber, forcing it into his hand. "No heroics. You need it as much as we do."

Connor drank the last dregs, the warm water wetting his mouth but doing little more. Only now did it hit him that they were in a survival situation.

Running from the gunmen was just the start of their problems. The main threat to their lives came from being in the wilds of Africa without food, water or weapons.

Colonel Black's parting words rang in his ears: *It's always best to be prepared for the worst, especially in Africa.* In light of their current situation, Connor thought that the colonel had never said truer words, and he wished now he'd spent more time studying the SAS survival handbook he'd been given.

Recalling that the right equipment could make the difference between life and death, Connor emptied his go-bag and took stock of their resources. He'd lost the most crucial item—his smartphone—back at the crash site, but he did have a small first-aid kit, empty water bottle, binoculars, malaria tablets, sunblock, insect repellent, a flashlight, a single energy bar, sunglasses with night-vision capability and, still attached to his belt, his father's knife.

"What's that?" asked Henri, pointing to a blue tube in the bottom of the bag.

Connor fished it out and smiled, glad of Bugsy's foresight. "A LifeStraw," he explained. "We just need to find water and we can all drink safely."

With one key survival factor half solved, Connor asked, "What do you have in your pockets?"

Amber produced cherry-flavored lip balm, a packet of tissues and a hair band. Henri had a couple of pieces of candy and his inhaler. Hiding his disappointment at such meager offerings, Connor opened the energy bar and divided it between the three of them. "Not much of a dinner, I'm afraid, but it's better than nothing."

The granola bar was gone in one bite, only serving to remind them of how hungry they were.

"Is this edible?" Connor asked, half joking, as he picked up the lip balm.

"Tastes nice and keeps your lips soft," replied Amber, "but not an ideal dessert."

Henri offered his two sweets to Connor and his sister.

"Save them," said Connor, smiling at his generosity. "We'll be needing them for breakfast."

Dusk was falling fast. Even with his night-vision sunglasses and a small flashlight, Connor knew that it would be foolish to navigate the jungle at night.

"We need to find a safe place to sleep," he said, repacking everything into his go-bag.

"We're not going back to the lodge?" Henri asked with an anxious glance at the gloomy jungle surrounding them.

Connor shook his head. "Too dangerous. It's best we hole up somewhere until daw—"

A rustle in the bushes alerted Connor to something approaching. He put a finger to his lips, urging Amber and Henri to remain silent.

The rustling drew closer. To Connor's ears, it sounded like more than one person, all converging on the ridge. The gunmen had caught up with them fast! But no doubt they had trackers with them.

Looking for a place to hide, he hustled Amber and Henri into a crevice in the rocks. They lay flat, waiting for the gunmen's approach. Reaching for his belt, Connor unsheathed his father's knife. Although it was no match for an assault rifle, he gained strength and courage from having it in his grasp.

The noise grew louder. Connor could hear Amber's panicked breathing in his ear and feel Henri's body trembling at his side. His grip on the knife tightened as a bush only a few feet away began to shake. Then a snout with two large curved tusks appeared, followed by a large flattened head and a gray bristled body. Snorting, a warthog trotted over the ridge, followed by a litter of young piglets.

Connor relaxed his grip on the knife and slowly let out the breath he'd been holding. The warthog suddenly turned her head in their direction. Sniffing the air, she grunted furiously, flattened her mane of bristles and bolted away, her piglets squealing in terror as they too ran for cover.

Amber laughed, more in relief than anything. "I'm glad there's something in this jungle more scared than we are!" she said.

But as they crawled out of the crevice, they discovered what the warthog and her piglets had really been running from.

The **B🗡DYGUARD** Missions

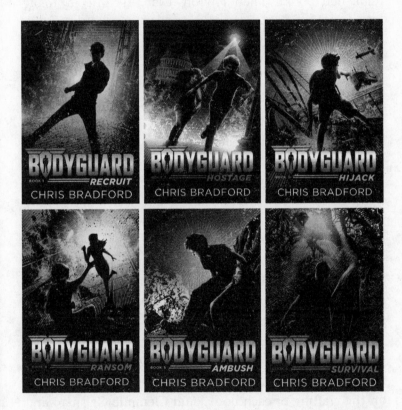

ACKNOWLEDGMENTS

Ambush is my eleventh full-length novel. My twenty-first published book! When I wrote that first line in *Young Samurai: The Way of the Warrior* back in 2006, I never dreamed that it would take me on such a long and incredibly rewarding journey. And with so much action and adventure ahead in the Bodyguard series, I need to thank those who have helped get me this far and will, I hope, continue to carry me into the future . . .

First and foremost, my wife, Sarah—yes, this was perhaps the least stressful of all the books I have written. Who knows, one day I might actually be "normal" when I'm writing a book! My two awesome sons, Zach and Leo—my reward is getting to play and have fun with you at the end of each day. My mum and dad, my first readers—I value all you do for me. Sue and Simon for your constant support. Steve and Sam for just being lovely and a rocking uncle and aunt to our boys! And Karen, Rob, Thomas and Benjamin for being there for us at all times.

It goes without saying that none of this would have been possible without my dear friend and agent, Charlie Viney. Pippa Le Quesne, thank you as ever for your guidance on the crafting of each book. And Clemmie Gaisman and Nicky Kennedy at ILA for conquering the world, territory by territory.

My Puffin team in the UK for their sterling work in beating my manuscripts into submission and producing a hardened warrior of a read by the end: Tig Wallace, my awesome editor; Helen Gray, my razor-sharp copy editor;

and Wendy Shakespeare, my constant star in the whole process.

On the other side of the pond, I have my American bodyguard team at Philomel to thank: Brian Geffen, my illustrious editor; Michael Green, my publisher; Laurel Robinson, my copy editor; designers Kelley Brady and Jennifer Chung and cover artist Tracie Ching for producing the stunning cover and interior designs for the US edition.

Authors Abroad are a crucial linchpin of the team organizing all my tours—so a big thank-you to Trevor Wilson and Shelley Lee (especially!), whose attention to detail and brilliant logistical skills make my touring life very easy.

My constant friends (young and old) Geoff, Lucy, Matt, Charlie, Russell, Hayley, Mark and my goddaughter Lulu, plus the members of the HGC to whom this book is dedicated: Dan, Siggy, Larry, Kul, Andy, Dax, David, Giles, Riz and any other poor unfortunate souls who might join our clan . . .

But the most important people to thank are you, my readers, for following both the Young Samurai and Bodyguard series, telling your friends and family about the books and posting reviews online. Without you, there would be no point in writing. So thank you for reading!

Stay safe.
Chris

Any fans can keep in touch with me and the progress of the Bodyguard series on my Facebook page or via the website at www.bodyguard-books.com.

© Rune Hellestad

Chris Bradford (www.chrisbradford.co.uk) is a true believer in "practicing what you preach." For his BODYGUARD series, Chris embarked on an intensive close-protection course to become a qualified professional bodyguard. His best-selling books, including the Young Samurai series, are published in more than twenty languages and have garnered more than thirty children's book award nominations internationally. He is a dedicated supporter of teachers and librarians in their quest to improve literacy skills and provides free teachers' guides to his books on his website. He lives in England with his wife and two sons.

Follow Chris on Twitter @youngsamurai.

AN INTERVIEW WITH CHRIS BRADFORD

What inspired you to set *Ambush* in Africa?

I lived for a short while in Africa and have done some charity work out there and it's a fantastically rich place in which to set an adventure. I wanted to give Connor and the bodyguards a new challenge, which involved protecting their principals not only from a legitimate threat, like gunmen in this instance, but also from the wilds of Africa. From my experience of being in Africa, it's a fantastic continent, but it's also a very dangerous one and I wanted to bring out those survival skills in Connor.

How did you go about researching *Ambush* and the dangers Connor faces?

I had the personal experience of encountering lions, scorpions and snakes so I've used those experiences, but I've also researched these animals too. I looked at the most dangerous creatures—for example, crocodiles, hippos and mosquito—and the ways to overcome them from a survival point of view, if you've got nothing around you.

Connor has to combat his fear of snakes in *Ambush*. What would you be most afraid of encountering?

My worst nightmare is sharks. I get a shiver of fear even if I just see a picture of one! You do see them in Africa but only on the coast. In the chapters where Amber encounters the spider, I used my own phobia of sharks to describe her paralyzing fear.

What are your top three tips for surviving in the African bush?

The three basics of survival are water, food and shelter. Without these, your chances of staying alive for any period of time are seriously reduced.

1. FIND WATER

In the savannah, it might not rain for weeks or even months. This makes finding water a difficult task, but there are ways:

- Search for animal tracks and follow them to see if they lead to water.
- If you find a fast-moving river, you're in luck. Beware stagnant streams and rivers, as these can harbor parasites and bacteria.
- If possible, boil any water you find to make it safe to drink.
- If you don't find water, dig at the lowest part of a river. Often water lies beneath the surface of a dried-up riverbed.

♦ If you do find water, use a piece of clothing to act as a sponge and trickle the water into your mouth.

2. FIND FOOD

Food can also be difficult to source, but if you find water then you'll likely find food nearby too. Berries and fruit might be your easiest and most abundant source of nutrition, but, before eating any, it's crucial to check if they're poisonous or not:

♦ First, cut open the fruit and smell it. If it smells like peaches or almonds, it's poisonous.

♦ Rub the fleshy part of the fruit on your skin and wait at least a minute to see if it produces a rash or reaction. If so, it's poisonous. Discard it.

♦ Next, touch the fruit to your lips. If you feel a burning sensation, the fruit is not safe to eat.

♦ Otherwise, move the fruit to your tongue but don't swallow. If the fruit doesn't aggravate your tongue, take a bite of the fruit and wait several hours to see if you become sick. If not, the fruit is edible.

In addition, good sources of protein are termites or larvae!

3. FIND SHELTER

To sleep safely at night:

♦ Make a boma—a circular enclosure of acacia branches. The thorns will keep nocturnal predators away.

- Climb a tree and tie yourself securely to the bough.
- Find a hollowed-out baobab tree to take refuge inside.
- Or climb up to a wide rock ledge and secure yourself so you don't roll off in the night.

The key factor is to keep out of reach of any potential predators while sleeping at night.

AFRICA'S DEADLIEST PREDATORS—
AND HOW TO SURVIVE THEM

1. LIONS

♦ Lions are the second-largest big-cat species in the world, after tigers.

♦ Adult males can eat up to ninety-seven pounds of meat in one sitting! How much do you weigh?

♦ A lion's roar can be heard from five miles away.

♦ Equipped with teeth that tear effortlessly through bone and tendon, lions can take down an animal as large as a bull giraffe. Once grabbed, the prey is subdued and suffocated with a quick neck bite or a sustained bite over the muzzle.

How to Survive a Lion Attack: If you encounter a lion, never turn your back and try to run. That is a death warrant. Your best chance is to stand still, stretch out your arms to look as large as possible, and try to outface the lion!

2. NILE CROCODILES

♦ A crocodile can snap its jaws shut, trapping prey within fifty milliseconds.

♦ Crocodiles have the strongest bite of any animal in the world. The muscles that open the jaws, however, aren't so powerful. A reasonably strong person could hold a crocodile's jaws closed with their bare hands!

♦ Each crocodile jaw has twenty-four teeth that are meant to grasp and crush, not chew. They swallow stones to grind food inside their stomachs.

♦ "Crying crocodile tears"—displaying fake sadness—comes from the myth that the reptiles weep when eating humans. They do wipe their eyes when feeding, but only because their eyes bubble and froth when eating.

How to Survive a Crocodile Attack: Most victims never see the crocodile coming. If caught in its jaws, trying to pull free is usually futile and may induce the crocodile to go into an underwater death roll. The only hope of survival is to fight back: hit or poke the eyes, the most vulnerable part of a crocodile's body. If that fails, strike the nostrils or ears. As a last-ditch attempt, go for the palatal valve—a flap of tissue behind the tongue that covers the crocodile's throat and prevents the animal from drowning. If your arm is stuck in a crocodile's mouth, you may be able to prize this valve down; water will then flow into the crocodile's throat, and hopefully it will let you go.

3. BLACK MAMBAS

♦ The fastest snake in the world, the black mamba is capable of moving at speeds of up to twelve miles per hour for short distances.

- Its venom is highly toxic. Two drops of venom can kill a person, and a mamba can have up to twenty drops in its fangs.
- The black mamba gets its name because of the black color inside its mouth (its body is usually olive brown).
- It is easily identified by its length (7.9 feet, average), slenderness, speed of movement and its coffin-shaped head.
- The black mamba has a reputation for being very aggressive.

How to Survive a Black Mamba Attack: Untreated bites are fatal. Put a tourniquet above the puncture wound to slow the spread of poison and seek medical attention immediately. The sooner a person is treated with antidote after the bite, the better the chances of survival.

4. HIPPOS

- Extremely aggressive if threatened, the hippo is responsible for more human fatalities in Africa than any other large animal.
- Hippos can easily outrun a human, reaching up to thirty miles per hour.
- Hippos can kill crocodiles.
- The most common threat display is the yawn, which is telling you to back off!
- An overheated hippo looks as if it is sweating blood; glands in its skin secrete a sticky red fluid that acts as a natural sunscreen.

How to Survive a Hippo Attack: Never get between a hippo and water. It makes them panic, which causes them to charge. Most human deaths happen because people surprise hippos accidentally.

5. LEOPARDS

♦ Built for hunting, leopards have sleek, powerful bodies and can run at speeds of up to thirty-five miles per hour.

♦ Leopards are also excellent swimmers and climbers, and they can jump long distances.

♦ Mostly nocturnal, leopards hunt prey at night. A common tactic is to leap out of trees onto their victim.

♦ Leopards protect their food from other animals by dragging it up into a tree. A male leopard can drag a carcass three times its own weight—including small giraffes—fifty feet up a tree!

♦ A leopard's characteristic call is a deep, rough cough, repeated ten to fifteen times, sounding like a saw cutting wood. An aggressive charge is heralded by two or three short coughs.

How to Survive a Leopard Attack: You probably won't!